The Mingrelian Conspiracy

By the same author

The Mingrelian Conspiracy

A Mamur Zapt Mystery

Michael Pearce

Poisoned Pen Press

Copyright © 1995 by Michael Pearce

U.S. First Trade Paperback Edition 2005

10 9 8 7 6 5 4 3 2 1

Library of Congress Catalog Card Number: 2003104878

ISBN: 1-59058-177-6 Trade Paperback

Poisoned Pen Press
6962 E. First Ave. Ste. 103
Scottsdale, AZ 85251
www.poisonedpenpress.com
info@poisonedpenpress.com

Printed in the United States of America

Chapter 1

'Once upon a time there was a woman called Rice Pudding and—'

'One moment,' said the Chief of the Secret Police: 'Rice Pudding?'

'Yes. And one day she was sitting at her window—'

'Rice Pudding?' said the Chief of Police warningly.

'It was a long time ago,' said the storyteller defensively.

'Very well. Proceed.'

'And suddenly she saw, down in the street below, a dervish looking very important and wearing round his neck a huge necklace made of the spouts off clay water jars strung together like beads. "What do you have for sale?" she called down to him. "Names," he said. "How much does a name cost?" "A hundred piastres." Now—'

'Perhaps you could just tell me,' suggested the Chief of Police, 'where you had got to?'

'He had got to the bit,' said one of the bystanders helpfully, 'when she had lost her new name and a blind man had found it and tied it up in a sack—'

'Hey!' said the storyteller angrily. 'Who's telling the story? You or me?'

'And was just about to carry it up the stairs—'

'When Mustapha cried out,' said the constable excitedly, unable to keep quiet any longer.

'Mustapha?' said the Chief of the Secret Police, who was having difficulties.

'From inside the café! I heard him!'

'Mustapha is the man who was injured?'

'That's right, Effendi! While we were listening to the story.'

'And I heard the cry,' said the constable. 'Oh, Effendi, it was a terrible cry! So I rushed at once into the café—'

'No, you didn't!' objected someone.

'Ahmed, are you looking for trouble?'

'I'm only saying you didn't rush in. You stayed right where you were.'

'We all did,' said someone else. 'It was a terrible cry.'

The crowd was pressing forward, eager to help.

'And then Leila called for help!'

'And we all rushed in—'

'Led by me,' said the constable swiftly.

'And found Mustapha lying there.'

'Right!' said the Chief of the Secret Police. 'So we're not in the story now; we're in what really happened?'

'Yes, Effendi, that's right. And there was Mustapha, lying in a pool of blood—'

Owen sighed. 'What really happened' was always a relative matter in Cairo. There had been, for instance, no pool of blood. The proprietor of the café had had his legs broken, which was the usual penalty for noncompliance when the gangs made their initial request. He glanced back over his shoulder.

'Where is Mustapha now?' he asked.

'Upstairs, Effendi. The hakim is with him.'

'Right. Well, I am going in to have a talk with him. In private. So you can all go home. There'll be nothing for you to see. No more excitement.'

He knew, however, that his words were wasted. The crowd would stay on in the hope of further drama at least until he left and probably long after.

'Keep them out,' he said to the constable. 'I don't want any company.'

'Right, Effendi!' said the constable, taking out his baton with alacrity. When Owen had arrived, the first thing he had had to do was clear the café of all sightseers, which meant the whole neighbourhood. They were all now packed in the street outside, which was jammed from one end to the other. The constable stationed himself in front of the entrance and swung his arm.

'Oy!' said someone indignantly. 'What do you think you're doing?'

'That'll teach you, Ahmed!' said the constable, grinning.

Owen gave him a warning look and then went inside. The café had obviously started life as a traditional Arab one and there were still stone benches round the walls with low tables in front of them and a rack of hose-stemmed bubble pipes in one corner. An attempt was being made, however, to take it up market. The central part of the floor was occupied by standard wooden European chairs and tables and scattered around were various European fixtures and fittings: a large gilt mirror, for instance, which might have strayed out of an East London pub. The density of the chairs and tables, and the fact that the café could afford a storyteller, suggested that it was popular. Just the kind of place, thought Owen, to attract the attention of the gangs.

A flight of stairs led upwards to the family's living quarters. In one of the rooms Owen found a cluster of people around a rope bed on which a man was lying. He had his trousers off and a man in a dark suit and fez was bending over him. A woman, unveiled, was wiping his face with a cloth.

'You wouldn't listen, would you?' she said.

The man ignored her. The doctor saw Owen and straightened up.

'Another one,' he said.

'Just the legs?'

'A smack or two in the face.'

'They broke my nose,' the man on the bed said, putting up his hand to feel his face. 'The bastards!'

The doctor inspected him critically.

'It'll be all right,' he said, 'when the swelling goes down. Your mouth will want some repair work, though. A couple of teeth have gone.'

The man felt gingerly inside his mouth with one finger and then sat bolt upright.

'It's the gold one! Leila, look in my mouth. It's the gold one, isn't it?'

The woman wiped the blood away and peered.

'It looks like it,' she said.

'Then where is it?'

'It'll be on the floor somewhere.'

'Go down and look for it! At once! Before any of those other bastards finds it and makes off with it!'

The woman hurried out of the room.

'Bastards!' said the man, lying back.

Owen moved forward.

'How do you feel?' he asked sympathetically.

'Bad!' said the man, without opening his eyes.

'I'll come and see you tomorrow,' said Owen, 'and we can talk more. But there's something I need to know quickly. The men; what were they like?'

The man was silent.

'You must have seen them,' insisted Owen.

The man looked up, as if registering his presence for the first time.

'Yes,' he said slowly, 'I saw them, all right.'

'Recognize any of them?'

'No. As soon as I saw the clubs I knew what I was in for, though.'

'Can you give me a description?'

'What's the use?' said the man.

'Scars?'

'Sudanis, you mean? Well, it might have been. We've got enough around.' He reflected a moment, then shook his head. 'It all happened so fast.'

'Were they wearing galabeeyahs? Or trousers?'

Some of the gangs were westernized. It might help to narrow the field.

'Do you know,' said the man, 'I can't remember. I really can't remember.'

☙

'Another one who won't talk?' The army major pursed his lips. 'We need to take a tougher line.'

'It's the only way.'

The speaker was new to the committee. Paul, in the chair, raised his eyebrows.

'Captain—?'

'Shearer,' said the major, introducing. 'Just joined us. The Sirdar thought he might be useful. Experience with Arabs. The Gulf. Knows how to handle them.'

'Bedouin?' said Paul. 'I think you may find the urban Egyptian a little different, Captain Shearer.'

'They're all the same.'

'I bow to your experience. And how long is it that you've been in Cairo?'

'I arrived last week,' said Shearer, flushing slightly.

'It's true, though,' insisted the major. 'They *are* all the same. Stick a knife through you as soon as look at you. I mean, that's what this meeting is about, isn't it? Stopping them getting hold of guns.'

'It's true that we have reason to suppose that some of the money the gangs collect through their protection rackets finds its way to the purchase of guns,' said Paul.

'Well, there you are, then. And we know who they'll be used against!'

'Armed uprising,' said the third member of the Army team loyally.

'Armed uprising?' said Owen incredulously. 'Do you know what the scale of this is?'

'Bloody vast,' said the major.

'Infinitesimal. There are less than a dozen gangs and fewer than twenty men in each. Two hundred men. Out of a population in the city of eight hundred thousand!'

'If there are so few,' said the major, 'why don't you get on top of them?'

Paul sighed.

'Operating in a city is not quite like operating against a few armed tribesmen in the desert,' he said.

'There I have to disagree with you,' said the new man, Captain Shearer. 'I think some of the lessons we've learned in the Gulf are very applicable in Cairo.'

'Quite right,' said the major approvingly.

'What had you in mind?' asked Owen. 'Machine guns?'

'Not quite that,' said Shearer. 'Although I do think you shouldn't underrate the part machine guns could play in dealing with mass disturbance in the squares. No, what I was thinking of was armed patrols on the streets—'

'There's hardly a need for that,' said Owen. 'It's a peaceful city.'

'People getting their legs broken?' said the major. 'I'd hardly call that peaceful.'

'You've got to see it in proportion.'

'The trouble is,' said Shearer, 'the proportion can very soon change if you don't stamp on this kind of thing at once.'

'Armed patrols?' said Owen. 'For God's sake!'

'From what I've seen,' said Paul, 'especially on the nights after they've been paid, it's the soldiers who are responsible for half the trouble!'

'I won't deny there's been the odd spot of bother recently,' said the major defensively.

'Actually, sir,' said Shearer, turning eagerly towards him, 'that rather supports the point I was making last night.'

'Oh, yes?' said the major vaguely.

'About unifying the policing of the city. The need to deploy more Military Police and bring security under a single command, preferably military—'

'What are you suggesting?' said Paul. 'Putting Cairo under military law?'

'Well—'

'Or are you merely saying that since the Army is responsible for most of the criminal violence that there is in the city, it should do something about it?'

'Well, I wouldn't put it quite like that—'

'He's right, though,' said the major doggedly. 'There ought to be a crackdown.'

Paul began to gather up his papers.

'Well, thank you, gentlemen. It's always a pleasure to hear the views of the Army. And most helpful to have a new contribution! I'm sure you're right, Captain Shearer, we all have much to learn. I'm afraid you'll find, though, when you've been here a little longer, that the situation in Egypt is not quite as straightforward as you suppose. Nor is Egyptian police work.'

⚬↝↜↝↝↜⚬

No, indeed. To start with the question of what the British were doing in Egypt anyway: they were there, they said, by invitation of the ruler of Egypt, the Khedive, to help him sort out the country's chaotic finances. True, the invitation had been nearly thirty years before and they were still there; but then, the finances were very complicated. True, too, that their help now extended very widely. There was a British adviser alongside every minister. There were Englishmen at the head of the police and the Army. And the British Consul-General was always there to advise the Khedive. But then, it was hard to separate finance from the general running of the country, as the Khedive soon sadly discovered.

It was true, however, that a number of people in Egypt, and most certainly the Khedive, had come to feel that the help was no longer necessary. But then, as Nationalist newspapers frequently observed, a growing number of Egyptians felt that the Khedive was no longer necessary either.

The situation was indeed not straightforward. Egypt had in effect two governments, the formal one of the Khedive and the shadow one of the British administration. In these circumstances a certain dexterity was required of administrators.

It was particularly required of the Mamur Zapt, a post traditional to, and peculiar to, Cairo. Broadly, Owen was responsible for what was coming to be known as security. In England the nearest equivalent was Head of the Political Branch of the Criminal Investigation Department. In Egypt the Mamur Zapt was traditionally thought of as Head of the Sultan's Secret Police. There was now no Sultan and, as a matter of fact, no Secret Police either; but views were slow to change.

Owen was, then, answerable for security. But answerable to whom? It was a question asked frequently by the Khedive and occasionally by the Consul-General and Owen never quite found the right answer. Khedive and Consul both agreed, however, that his duties should be carried out so discreetly as not to cause trouble. Owen was in favour of this, too, very much so, only it was not always easy to achieve in this city of sixty nationalities, most of whom were always at each other's throats, one hundred and twelve different ethnic groups, ditto, two hundred plus sects of a variety of religions, even more ditto, and growing Egyptian nationalism. Not to mention the fact that there was not one but three legal systems, each with its own courts, among which agile criminals could slip with eternal impunity.

No, indeed, policing in Egypt was not straightforward, thought Owen, as he sat benignly in a café at that corner of the Ataba-el-Khadra where the Musky debouches into the square. That stupid meeting with the Army had taken up so much of the morning that he had been obliged to go back to his office in the afternoon, which, at this time of the year, very few people did. Throughout the morning the heat built up so that, despite the closed shutters and the whirling fans, by noon everybody was wilting. They clung nobly on till about one o'clock, or, in the case of the British, eager to demonstrate both the heaviness of their workload and their superiority to the elements, two o'clock, and then thankfully packed it in for the day and went home for their siesta. Owen could never sleep during the day and usually went to the baths at this time to have a swim while the pool was empty. Not infrequently he then went back to the office and stayed there until the twilit hour when the day suddenly cooled and all the cafés came alive. Then he headed for a nearby one, along with half the population of Cairo.

There were, he had long ago decided, two stages. In the first, people woke up from their siesta, stretched themselves and thought that a little air would do them good. They went out into the street and found by some strange coincidence that everyone else was doing the same. They strolled along together, every few steps stopping to greet acquaintances, until the sun dropped below the minarets and suddenly the thought struck them how pleasant it would be to step aside for a moment and take a little coffee in one of those tiny cafés that, conveniently, cropped up every few yards in Cairo. Indeed, Cairo seemed at times one continuous café. They would sit there chatting and watching the world go by— since most of the tables were outside—until the time came for dinner, when they would rise, shake hands with the entire café, and depart.

The second stage followed immediately afterwards, when people would arise from their evening meal, feel the need for a breath of air, go outside and in no time at all finish up in a café, where they would remain for the rest of the evening. Life in the hot season was best lived out of doors, Cairenes were naturally sociable people, and the café world took over.

There, if you sat long enough, you would meet everyone you wanted to see. Take that fat Greek, for instance, about to drop into a chair a few tables away; Owen had been wanting to talk to him for days.

He waved a hand. The Greek came over and joined him.

'Where have you been?'

'Checking out possible places.'

'It's a bit hit-and-miss.'

'You get a feel.'

'Any particular feels?'

'Well—' said Georgiades, looking round evasively for the waiter.

'I've been thinking. Maybe the best chance we've got is catching them at the start of the process. You know, after the first visit.'

'After they've left their visiting card? It's a bit late then, isn't it? People might be even less inclined to talk.'

'At least we'd have something to go on. Now, in fact, there was a place yesterday—'

'Jesus!' said Georgiades, scrambling up. 'It's Rosa!'

A very young, thin slip of a girl was standing beside them, arms akimbo, eyes blazing.

'I thought you were supposed to be meeting me?'

She gestured towards a pile of packages on the pavement.

'On my way! I was on my way!'

'You were sitting here. He spends all his time these days,' she said to Owen, 'sitting in cafés.'

'I was working!' protested Georgiades.

'In a café? Since when is sitting in a café work?'

'It's what all the bosses do,' said Georgiades. 'As soon as they get anywhere, that's what they do. Sit down in a café all day.'

'Yes, but you haven't got anywhere yet.'

'I'm anticipating,' said Georgiades.

Owen felt the need to intervene on his behalf.

'It's my fault, really,' he said. 'I caught his eye—'

'He was going to sit down anyway,' said Rosa. 'Before he saw you. I was watching.'

'You were watching?' said Georgiades. He turned to Owen. 'Hey, she ought to be in this business, not me!'

'Why don't you join us?' suggested Owen. 'You must be tired after carrying all that lot. Tell you what, you sit down and have a cup of coffee, and I'll pay for an arabeah to take you home.'

'Well—' said Rosa, weakening.

But only for a moment.

'Take us both home,' she stipulated. 'I don't want to carry all these damned packages up the stairs. Besides,' she said generously, 'he'll be tired after all this work he's been doing.'

Owen held a chair for her. Rosa sat down, pleased. She had a soft spot for Owen. In fact, she told herself, she might well have decided to marry him, not Georgiades, at the time of the wretched business of her father's kidnapping, had she not known about him and Zeinab. Rosa stood rather in awe of Zeinab, not because she was a great lady, the daughter of a Pasha, no less, but because she had somehow solved, or seemed to have solved, the problem of being an independent woman in a man's world. She took Zeinab secretly as her model. Zeinab, for instance, would have made no bones about sitting down in this café, populated as it was entirely by men. Rosa sat and lifted her chin.

She could only, Owen thought, be about sixteen even now. She had married Georgiades (and this was exactly the way to put it, since he had not had much say in the matter) when she was only fourteen. Rosa had sworn blind that she was fifteen, although her parents had been equally convinced that she was fourteen. Fourteen was, in any case, quite allowable in Cairo and Rosa had received unexpected support from her grandmother, who was a little vague about when she herself had married but thought it was young and thoroughly approved Rosa's following tradition. This was exactly what Rosa had no intention of following. Her grandmother would certainly not have approved of her sitting here; which made it, of course, all the more enjoyable.

'He really is working, you know, when he's in these cafés,' said Owen, determined to do his best for Georgiades.

Rosa nodded, and then thought. She was as sharp as a knife, an implement which she had threatened to use on Georgiades if she caught him straying, and it didn't take her long to work out that two and two make four.

'It's protection, is it?' she said. 'The cafés?'

Rosa knew all about the protection racket. Her family had a business. They dealt in such things as lacquered boxes, old jewellery, Assiut shawls and ancient Persian amulets. One day the gangs had called.

'You're going about it the wrong way,' she said. 'Sending him round the cafés. They'll be too frightened to talk. You've got to be able to offer them something.'

'We *are* offering them something: defence.'

Rosa shook her head.

'It's too risky,' she said. 'You might catch the gang, you might not. If you don't, and they've talked to you, then they're in trouble. Why take a chance?'

'Because otherwise they have to pay. And go on paying.'

'You ought to go about it in a different way. Don't let them think they're talking to you. Why don't you have him go round pretending to sell insurance? Insurance against loss? They'll all be interested in that. They'll want to know what it covers. It would at least get them talking. And then he might be able to lead them on. He's good,' said Rosa, looking unforgivingly at the pile of packages beside her, 'at leading people on.'

ᏬᎷᏬᎤᎩ

Owen sent them off in an arabeah, the universal one-horse cab of Cairo, and settled down to wait for the bill. You could wait a long time for that and meanwhile his eyes wandered relaxedly over the scene in front of him. The Ataba-el-Khadra was the meeting place of two worlds. The Musky led straight up from the Old City and you went down it if you were a European wanting to visit the bazaars, or came up it if you were a native intending to visit the shops in the European quarter or, more likely, catch a tram. The Ataba was the terminus for most of Cairo's tram routes and at any hour of the day or night the square was full of trams, native horse-drawn buses, arabeahs and camels bringing forage for the horses. It was also full of street hawkers selling brushes (why?), ice-cream, lemonade, water, sponges, loofahs, canes (no young effendi from one of the big offices was properly dressed unless he carried a cane), hats (the pot-like tarboosh of the Egyptian) and sugar for instant consumption. The two biggest industries, however, were selling pastries and selling Nationalist newspapers. Cairenes, lacking confidence, perhaps, in their public-transport system, believed in stocking up before embarking on a journey. But they also believed in not making a journey at all but just sitting around, and when they sat around, they liked to sit in a café and read scurrilous Nationalist newspapers. Just behind the Ataba were the big offices of Credit Lyonnais and the Mixed Tribunals and beyond them the headquarters of the Anglo-Egyptian Bank, and the countless young men who worked in them were all avid Nationalists.

Owen looked around at the crowded café and thought: if other cafés, why not this one?

He knew the proprietor of the café and beckoned him over.

'Tell me, Yasin,' he said. 'Do you pay protection?'

'Not yet,' said the proprietor.

'Is that because they have not asked? Or because you have not agreed?'

'If they asked,' said Yasin, diplomatically but evasively, 'I would reply: I need no protection, for the Mamur Zapt sits every night at my tables.'

The first stage of the café evening was coming to an end and at several tables people were standing up and shaking hands. It was time to be firm about that bill. Or perhaps, just before he left, an apéritif?

'How about an apéritif?' said a familiar voice, and Paul dropped into a chair beside him.

'I reckon you owe me one,' said Owen, 'after that meeting this morning.'

'Bloody awful, wasn't it? It's high time the Army went on manoeuvres. Preferably at the bottom of the Red Sea.'

'What's all this business about unifying the policing? I don't like the sound of it.'

'It won't get anywhere. The Old Man will kill it dead.'

Paul was one of the Consul-General's aides and frequently, as this morning, chaired meetings on his behalf.

'Will he, though? If they really push?'

'They'll only get his back up. He'll see it as trespassing.'

'Yes, but—'

'It won't get anywhere. At the end of the day, the Old Man's a politician, and the one empire politicians will really fight for is their own. You can go back to sleep.'

Paul sipped his apéritif.

'All the same,' he said reflectively, 'on something like this it might be best if you didn't.'

'The gangs?' Owen was surprised. 'I really don't think, Paul, you need worry too much about the guns. It's pretty small—'

'Guns?' said Paul, so steeped in the ways of the city that he considered himself a born-again Cairene. 'Who the hell cares about guns? It's the cafés I'm thinking of.'

Chapter 2

Later the same day Owen had moved on to the second stage of the café evening and was comfortably enjoying an after-dinner coffee outside a crowded Arab café when an orderly, who knew his habits, brought him a hurried message from the Deputy Commandant of Police. It said:

> *Can you get down to the Ezbekiyeh quick? Trouble at a café. I've got my hands full at the Citadel. McPhee.*

Trouble at a café, thought Owen. Christ, they're keeping on the go. But when he got to the place he found it was nothing to do with protection but just an ordinary common or garden incident such as disfigured Cairo's streets most weekends. The Ezbekiyeh contained a number of houses of ill repute and was much frequented by British soldiers. Opposite the balconies from which scantily dressed ladies suggested their all were some very low-class cafés in which yet insufficiently aroused clients could sit and gaze.

And drink. Which was exactly what a bunch of Welsh Fusiliers had been doing until they had spotted at the next café a group of the Duke of Cornwall's Light. Relations between the regiments were not cordial, a matter, apparently, of the condition in which the DCLI had once left some barracks when the Welsh were due to move in, and merry banter was exchanged. As the evening wore on, and more drink was consumed, the banter became less merry. Remarks were made which, the Welsh considered, reflected on their nation ('Couldn't kick a ball near the posts, never mind through them') and they had risen to defend theirs and their country's honour. In the ensuing fracas a surprising number of bottles had been broken and a considerable amount of furniture damaged; so, too, had been a considerable number of soldiers.

The police had been summoned and a constable had indeed arrived but had wisely confined himself to the role of a spectator. When he saw Owen he fell in—behind him—with considerable relief.

Owen had no great desire to get involved in a brawl either. He doubted very much if the contestants were in a condition in which they could respond to the voice of command, much less a civilian voice of command; and then what would he do? He advanced slowly down the street towards them.

The fighting seemed, fortunately, to have reached a slight lull. Those still on their feet paused for a moment, breathing heavily. They were just about to resume, however, when a voice came sharply from the other end of the street: 'Stop that at once!'

The combatants looked up, surprised.

A slight, smartly dressed man came out of the darkness towards them.

'Stop that at once! Stand apart!'

'Blimey!' said one of the soldiers incredulously. 'A Gyppie!'

'Bloody hell!'

''Ere,' said another voice, 'what do you think you're doing? Ordering us around?'

'He needs bloody straightening out.'

'He bloody does!'

They began to move towards him.

Owen, in a fury now, and forgetting himself, started forward. 'Cut that out! None of that! Get back! Get back at once!'

'Christ!' said one of the soldiers. 'Here's another one!'

'He's bloody British, though.'

'I *am* bloody British,' snapped Owen, 'and tomorrow morning I'll have you bloody lot on jankers. I'll have you bloody running round and round the parade ground until your bloody balls drop off—'

'He speaks a bit like an officer,' said one of the men doubtfully.

'What's he in civvies for?'

'Must be off duty.'

'—and drop on the ground and lie there till they fry—' raged Owen.

The men, impressed, stopped fighting.

'That was lovely!' said one of the Welshmen. 'A bit poetic!'

A group of men in uniform suddenly appeared at the end of the street.

'Christ!' said one of the soldiers. 'We're for it! It's the jelly-babies!'

'What's going on?' shouted a voice that was vaguely familiar.

The Military Police came down the street.

'What's going on?'

Owen recognized the voice now. It was Shearer.

'These men have been disturbing the peace,' said the Egyptian.

'Oh, have they? We'll soon see about that! Get their names, sergeant!'

'I would like a copy, please,' said the Egyptian.

'I beg your pardon?'

'It would save me having to do it for myself.'

'I'm handling them,' said Shearer. 'It's no concern of yours.'

'I'm afraid it is,' said the Egyptian.

'Oh?' said Shearer. 'And who the hell are you?'

'Can I introduce you?' said Owen, stepping forward. 'Mr. Mahmoud El Zaki, Captain Shearer. Mr. El Zaki is a member of the Parquet and is, presumably, the officer investigating this case.'

If so, it would be very speedy. In Egypt the police had no powers of investigation. They merely reported a case of suspected crime to the Department of Prosecutions of the Ministry of Justice, the Parquet, which then assigned one of its lawyers to conduct the investigation.

'There is no case,' said Shearer. 'It's an internal matter for the Army.'

'I'm afraid not,' said the Egyptian. 'Since the incident has been formally reported a file will have been already opened.'

'I suggest you close it, then.'

'That will not be possible.'

Shearer looked at Owen.

'I'm afraid he's right. Once the process has been formally initiated it rolls on until it's formally closed.'

'How do I go about getting it formally closed?'

'A request has to go in from the administration. Get your people to contact Paul Trevelyan.'

Shearer made a note of the name.

'He's the chap who was chairing the meeting this morning,' said Owen.

Shearer frowned.

'Meanwhile,' said Owen, pointedly, 'you are obliged to cooperate with the Parquet.'

'The names, please,' said the Egyptian.

Shearer gave in with an ill grace.

'Give him a copy when you've finished,' he said to the sergeant. 'You lot,' he said, turning on the soldiers, 'had better get back to barracks. You're a bloody disgrace. I'll deal with you in the morning.'

'Better send them separately,' advised Owen. 'Otherwise they'll start fighting again.'

'They'd better bloody not! You're right, though, it's best to make sure. You lot,' he said to the DCLI, 'get started.

Sergeant, take half your men and go with them. You shower,' he said to the Fusiliers, 'start in ten minutes. Corporal, see they don't cause any more trouble.'

'The list, sir,' said the sergeant, giving it to the Egyptian. He did not normally reckon to say 'sir' to Egyptians but this situation seemed a bit complicated, and then there was the other funny bloke standing by whom Shearer seemed to listen to.

'Thank you.' The Egyptian hesitated. 'Are you not going to take the names of witnesses?' he asked, puzzled. 'You spoke of Army legal processes.'

'Not necessary, I think,' said Shearer.

The Egyptian raised an eyebrow, then shrugged. He took out a notebook and went over to the owner of the Fusiliers' café.

'Will you want to talk to me?' asked Owen.

'If you wouldn't mind,' said the Egyptian, over his shoulder.

Shearer frowned.

'I don't think that's right,' he objected. 'You ought not to be called on to give evidence against our own people. It puts you in an awkward position.'

'Ah!' said Owen. 'I'm used to that!'

Shearer hesitated and then, as the Egyptian did not appear to be disposed to go at once to Owen, which was what Shearer half expected, said good night and went after the departed DCLI.

Owen found himself standing next to the Fusiliers.

'Excuse me, sir,' said one of them, recognizing a country-man. 'Where are you from?'

'Machen.'

'Are you, indeed, sir? I'm from Caerphilly.'

'And I'm from Llanbradach, sir,' put in another of the Fusiliers.

'I know it well,' said Owen.

'And I know Machen, sir. My aunt is Mrs. Roberts, of the Post Office, sir.'

'Mrs. Roberts?' It was a hundred years since Owen had been in Wales. But vague memories of his childhood began to stir. 'I remember her, I think. How is she?'

'Not very well, sir. She's getting on a bit now. She's more or less given up the Post Office. She leaves it mostly to Blodwen now.'

'Blodwen?'

'Her daughter, sir. You remember her?'

'I think I do. A tiny little thing?'

'Not so tiny, now, sir.'

'She's married, sir,' said another of the Fusiliers.

'Heavens! Well, it was a while ago. I left for India when I was eighteen.'

'We thought you'd been in the Army, sir. It was the way you spoke.'

The corporal came up.

'All right, you lot,' he said. 'On your way!'

'Sorry about the bother, sir,' said one of the Fusiliers as they left. 'Those English bastards called us Welsh bastards!'

'Well, there's no need for you to rise like a fish!'

'No, sir.' They sounded, however, unconvinced.

'Nice fishing at Machen, sir!' one of them called out as they left.

The Egyptian came across to Owen as soon as they were gone.

'Have I got it right?' he said. 'They are also from the *Pays de Galles?*'

Professional Egyptians, as well as upper-class Egyptians, tended to speak French more readily than they did English. Many of them had been to France for their education. Mahmoud El Zaki had not. He had done all his training in the Khedivial School of Law. The Egyptian legal system, however, was heavily based on the French and the whole legal culture was strongly French.

'That's right,' said Owen. 'It's a Welsh regiment.'

'I'm surprised you keep them together,' said the Egyptian. 'Isn't there the risk of rebellion?'

'No, no, no. It's not like that. The English conquest of Wales was so long ago that most people have forgotten it. Well, almost.'

The Egyptian was not entirely convinced.

'There seemed to me to be animosity,' he said. 'Those other men were English, yes? An English regiment?'

'Some Cornishmen might dispute it, but yes. The conquest of Cornwall was even longer ago than the conquest of Wales.'

The Egyptian shook his head in wonderment.

'I thought the British were all the same,' he said. 'Of course, I knew that you were from the *Pays de Galles*. You had told me. But I had thought that you were an exception. British is not English, then?'

'Oh, no. It is Welsh and Scottish and Irish and—'

'Cornish?'

'If you go far enough back. And other things as well.'

The Egyptian looked thoughtful.

'It sounds like Cairo to me.' He glanced at his watch. 'Look,' he said, 'I won't take up your time now. Why don't we have a coffee somewhere? Sidi Hassim's, in an hour's time?'

ഇ

The trouble with the Cairo late-night café culture was that after the evening came the morning. Sleeping outside in the garden, because of the heat, Owen habitually awoke with the sun, no matter what time he'd gone to bed the night before. The result was that he'd normally passed his peak for the day by about nine, which was, of course, when the committees usually began, and after that it was all downhill. This morning he was present in the flesh but fragile in the spirit.

'We're always having meetings,' he complained to Paul.

'Yes, I know,' said Paul, 'and we could do without this one. However, a formal request has come in, or is about to come in, from Captain Shearer which, I think, needs discussion.'

'Hasn't it come in yet?' said the major, equally fed up at having to be present. 'If it's not come in, why not wait until it does?'

'Because that would rule out some of the options open to us.'

'Such as?'

'Not putting in a formal request.'

'The Army does not change its mind,' said Shearer stiffly.

'Keeping it informal, you mean?' asked the major. 'Well, that's usually best. Keep things off paper.'

'I agree with you in principle, sir,' said Shearer. 'In fact, that's exactly what I tried to do last night. Only this other Johnny said that things had already got past that stage.'

'Who is the other Johnny?' asked Paul.

'Mahmoud,' said Owen.

'Mahmoud El Zaki? The Parquet's already involved? This makes it more difficult.'

'Presumably there was a complaint,' said Owen.

'Actually,' said McPhee, Deputy Commandant of the Cairo Police, present this morning, 'there were two.'

'And they've assigned an officer already? That's pretty quick off the mark!'

'I think they've got a duty-officer system,' said Owen, 'and Mahmoud was probably the lawyer on duty. Anyone else would have left it till morning.'

'It had to be Mahmoud!' said Paul, vexed.

'Difficult man, eh?' said the major.

'That was certainly my impression last night, sir,' said Shearer.

'Difficult?' said Paul. 'No. Conscientious.' He turned to Owen. 'You know Mahmoud,' he said. 'It was only last night. They can hardly have got started. Do you think that there's any chance—?'

'No,' said Owen. 'He'll see it as a matter of principle.'

'Well, it *is* a matter of principle,' said Shearer. 'Does the Army come under Egyptian law?'

'Can't have that!' said the major, aghast.

'I absolutely agree, sir,' said Shearer. 'And therefore I think the issue must be faced. Settle it once and for all. That was exactly my thinking last night. If the Johnnies want it formal, then let them have it formal; and see if they like the consequences!'

'Hear, hear!' said the major.

'Look,' said Paul, 'the only way we get by in Egypt is by *not* facing issues. We take damned good care to see that issues are *not* faced.'

'Chickening out!' said Shearer contemptuously.

'Damned shillyshallying!' said the major.

'And this is for a very good reason,' said Paul; 'the ground we stand on is shaky.'

'Not while the Army's here!' said Shearer.

'By God, no!' said the major.

'I'm thinking of the formal, legal grounds by which we justify our presence here.'

'Well,' said Shearer, 'I don't think we need to think too much about that. We're here, aren't we?'

'It's a question of how we appear in the eyes of other countries.'

'Other countries!' said the major dismissively.

'I agree, sir,' said Shearer. 'The Army will look after that!'

'One of the complaints,' said McPhee, 'came from the Russian Chargé.'

'Russian Chargé!' said Paul.

'Apparently the soldiers assaulted him.'

'God Almighty!' said Paul. 'It's already an international incident!'

'Gentlemen. We should not lose our heads—' began Shearer.

'Heads?' said Paul. 'Heads? And what do you think will happen to yours when the Commander-in-Chief, the Prime Minister back in London, learns that the country's been committed to war through the actions of a junior captain?'

'Perhaps we should think again,' said the major. 'Maybe it would be best after all if the whole thing was handled informally.'

'Too late,' said Paul. 'It's in the hands of the Parquet now. The Nationalists will have us over a barrel. They'll exploit it internationally. Even your ambassador can't walk along the street without being bloody jumped on by British soldiers.'

'We'll confine them to barracks,' said the major. 'Keep them off the streets for a time. Can't we hush this thing up?'

'Not a chance!' said Paul, beginning to enjoy himself. 'The Parquet's Nationalist. It's rubbing its hands at all the trouble it'll be able to cause.'

'It wouldn't be possible—would it—to get the Chargé to withdraw his complaint?' said the major desperately. 'I mean, they wouldn't be able to go ahead then, would they? They'd have to, well, drop it.'

Paul affected to consider.

'I could go and grovel to the Chargé, I suppose,' he said unwillingly.

'Well, look—'

'I could give it a go. There'd have to be a written apology, of course.'

'You could manage that, couldn't you?'

'It wouldn't have to be from me. It would have to be from you.'

'The Army?' The major swallowed; swallowed again. 'I think that could be arranged.'

'And Captain Shearer withdraws his request?'

'In the circumstances,' mumbled Shearer.

'Right, then!' said Paul, triumphant, beginning to gather his papers. 'We—'

'Excuse me,' said McPhee, the Deputy Commandant, with his usual slightly anxious old-world courtesy, 'haven't you forgotten something? There was another complaint.'

'My God!' said Paul. 'It's all Europe now!'

'No, no,' said McPhee seriously. 'It's not from the Diplomatic this time.'

'Who is it, then?'

'The leader of the Mingrelian community.'

There was a little silence.

'What did you say?'

'Mingrelian.'

'Oh, Mingrelian, Mingrelian!' said Paul, starting up. 'My God!' he said, catching Owen's eye, 'Mingrelian!'

'Mingrelian!' responded Owen loyally, seeing that something of the sort was required but not, however, having the faintest idea what it was all about, never, indeed, having heard of anything Mingrelian before. 'Mingrelian!' he said, shaking his head.

'Them above all!' said Paul, all dejection.

'Look,' said the major apprehensively, 'if they're a particularly difficult lot—'

'Difficult!' said Paul. 'Difficult! Not content with having provoked a world war, you bring out on to the streets the most bloodthirsty, intransigent—'

'Armed uprising?' said Shearer. 'We can handle them!'

'Both of them?' said Paul. 'At once?'

'We'll cope,' said the major. 'We'll cope.' He looked, however, distinctly worried. 'Two fronts,' he said. He shook his head. 'Don't like it,' he said.

'None of us like it,' said Paul bravely. 'We have to look issues in the face, though. There may be still time, however. I'll go straight to the Russian Chargé and grovel. Oh, no, wait a minute. First, we need a letter of apology.'

'I'll see to it,' said the major.

'Right. Then keep your men off the streets—'

'Lie low for a bit. Right, I get the picture,' said Shearer.

'And persuade the Army to refrain, at least for a time, from assaulting the minority of the population it hasn't so far assaulted.'

'Right,' said the major.

Paul looked pleased.

'That's it, then?'

'The complaint from the Mingrelians,' McPhee gently prompted.

'Ah, yes. Well,' said Paul, looking at Owen; 'something for the Mamur Zapt, isn't it?'

'Thanks very much,' said Owen.

⚬⚬⚬

'Paul,' he said worriedly, as they walked away together. 'Who the hell are the Mingrelians?'

'Don't ask me,' said Paul. 'Never heard of them.'

⚬⚬⚬

'Just bring me the Mingrelian file, will you?' said Owen casually, glancing up at Nikos as the Official Clerk entered the room.

'The what file?'

'Mingrelian.'

Nikos stood for a moment, stunned. He liked to claim he had a file on everything. He believed he had the universe under control. Now the earth had moved.

'Mingrelian. Oh yes, Mingrelian,' he said, recovering quickly. He stopped in the doorway. 'It may take a bit of time,' he warned.

'I'll bet,' said Owen.

Nikos went out grim-faced.

⚬⚬⚬

'Do you realize what you've done?' demanded Georgiades.

'He hasn't got a file!' chortled Owen.

'He'll have one soon. Those people were happily getting on with their lives unknown to the world. Now you've dragged them into history!'

'Ever heard of them?'

Georgiades rubbed his chin. There was a faint rasp. It was difficult to shave close in the heat.

'The name seems vaguely familiar. Something to do with the Church?'

* * *

'The Church!' said McPhee, shocked. 'Really, Owen! And you the son of a minister! It is true that they are members of the Orthodox communion at one remove, so to speak, since the Georgian Church is autocephalous—'

'Georgia? Is that where they come from?'

'The Caucasus, rather. They are a separate linguistic community. Linguistic, not religious. How could you think, Owen—?' said McPhee reproachfully.

* * *

Later in the morning Owen took pity on Nikos.

'There's been a complaint, apparently, about the behaviour of some British soldiers last night. It came from the leader of the Mingrelian community. Can you get me the details? At least the name.'

'The Parquet?'

'Yes.'

'I'll go directly to them,' said Nikos, straight-faced. 'It'll be quicker than finding the file.'

* * *

Owen guessed that he was getting near the place when he began to see increasing numbers of Albanians and Montenegrins standing about at street corners wearing national dress. It was not that the Caucasus was part of the Balkans, just that in Cairo certain groups of communities tended to stick together and the nationalities of the Eastern Mediterranean constituted one such group. Not all of them, however, insisted on wearing national dress. That was a peculiarity of the Albanians and Montenegrins, adopted, Owen thought, chiefly because it was a lot less strenuous to stand about all day in picturesque dress in front of the tourists' hotels charging for photographs than to work for a living. Anyway, they looked splendid chaps in their high boots and their billowing trousers and with a whole armoury stuck in their belts.

'The house of Sorgos?'

The Montenegrin thought for a moment and then took Owen familiarly by the arm and led him down a narrow alley and out into a small close of very old houses, so old that they were threatening to slide into each other and their heavy, wooden *meshrebiya* windows bowed down almost to the ground. The Montenegrin stopped before the door of one of them.

'The house of Sorgos,' he said, saluted and left.

Owen knocked on the door.

It was opened by one of the most beautiful women Owen had ever seen.

He was quite taken aback, firstly because he had expected the door to be opened by a servant—few houses were so poor as to be without a servant of some sort—and secondly because she was unveiled. He had grown so used to women being in veils that now he was disconcerted to see one without one. What sort of woman would come to the door without a veil on?

Not *that* sort of woman, he realized at once. This one was soberly dressed and serious looking.

'Yes?'

'The house of Sorgos?'

She nodded.

'Is he at home?'

'No. What is your business?'

'I am the Mamur Zapt. I would like to talk to him.'

'He is not at home,' she said, 'but he will be back soon. Would you like to come in?'

She led him into a small room sparely furnished in the Eastern style, with marble tiles on the floor and carpets on the walls. He sat down on a low divan with various bits of brassware on a table before him.

'I will bring some coffee.'

Unusually, there were books. They were scattered everywhere, on the tables, on the floor, in the little niches where there should have been pots, in piles against the walls.

'My father collects stories,' she said, pulling up a brazier and putting the pot down beside him.

'Collects them?'

'Yes. The original manuscripts if he can, early printed versions if he can't.'

'And they are to do with what?'

'Folk stories, epics, wonder tales.'

'*The Arabian Nights?*'

'He would like to think so. My father is in Paris now.'

'Buying?'

'Selling.'

'Oh!'

'He hates it. He hates parting. But obviously we have to live. And anyway, we have the story.'

'In what language?'

'Any language.'

'It was just that—you are Mingrelian, aren't you?'

'Yes.' She was a little surprised. 'How did you know? Oh, my grandfather!'

'You don't confine yourselves to stories of the Caucasus?'

'The Caucasus was long ago,' she said, 'and my grandfather does not like to talk about it. We have been in Cairo now for thirty years. Longer, even, than the British!'

The serious face suddenly dissolved. Owen was enchanted. But still uncomfortable.

'You are Christian, of course?'

'Of course.'

'I was missing the veil.'

'I do wear a veil when I go out. It saves trouble with the neighbours. But not at home.'

'Your grandfather allows you considerable freedom,' he observed.

It wasn't just the Muslims who liked to keep their women private. It was the Italians, the Greeks, the Levantines, the Albanians, all the Balkan countries. You could live in Egypt forever and never meet a single woman socially. Until he had met Zeinab, Owen had felt very deprived.

'He believes in freedom,' she said. 'That, of course, is why we left Russia. As they call our country now.'

'I hadn't realized there was such a community of you here.'

'Well, it isn't such a community really. There are only about sixty families. When you are as small as that you have to fight very hard in order to survive. Marriage becomes important. Children become important. You must not let the language die out.'

'And you? Are you married?'

She laughed.

'Not yet,' she said. 'The problem is, you have to marry a Mingrelian.'

'The trouble with freedom,' said Owen, 'is that it broadens the outlook.'

He heard someone come in through the outer door and rose to his feet.

'You have a visitor, Grandfather,' said the girl. 'The Mamur Zapt!'

An old man came into the room. Owen knew, of course, that he must be old; but that was not the immediate impression he gave. He had the same handsome features as the girl and his hair still retained some of the same striking black. He strode vigorously across the room and clasped Owen by the hand.

'The Mamur Zapt! To what do I owe this honour?'

'I have come to apologize,' said Owen, 'for the boorish behaviour of some British soldiers.'

The old man started to wave the issue away but then his hand stopped.

'Well,' he said, 'it was an insult, and the Mingrelians cannot accept insults. The Mingrelians above all! When you are a small community you have to fight. Otherwise they will break you down.'

'There is no desire in any way to do that. The Mingrelian community is much respected. The Sirdar and the Consul-General'—this was stretching it a bit—'have asked me to present their personal apologies. Those responsible will be sought out and punished.'

'It is the slight to our honour that must be redressed.'

'Quite so.'

'We are a small nation but we have our pride.'

'Absolutely.'

'Some would say we are not even a nation!'

'Oh, surely no one would say—'

'Well, they do. They do. They say, how can you be a nation when you haven't got a country? And I say, we had a country once, only it was taken from us. But, in any case, I say, a nation is more than land. It is spirit. And that spirit we, in our small way, must keep alive even in Cairo!'

'Absolutely!'

'And so,' said the old man, 'we must defend our honour!'

'Quite so,' said Owen, and then, more cautiously: 'up to a point.'

'No!' roared the old man, hammering his fist on the end of the divan. 'No! On honour there are no half measures!'

'It is right to resent an affront,' said Owen, 'but wrong, after an apology, to nurse a grievance. All that honour requires, surely, is recognition?'

'Surely courtesy requires recognition, too,' said the girl. 'And what has become of hospitality?'

The old man smote himself on the temple.

'She does right to remind me!' he said.

He went to sit down on the divan but then, with an apology, left it to Owen and sat down on another divan opposite him. The girl stirred the coffee and poured out two little cups, one for her grandfather, one for Owen.

'Both courtesy and hospitality,' said Owen, 'require thanks.'

The girl smiled at him and went out to replenish the coffee.

'A good girl,' said the old man, watching her fondly, 'and with a mind of her own! Just like her grandmother.' He shook his head sadly. 'A disappointment, though!'

'Oh, come—'

'No, no. It's true. Twenty-one and not married! In no time at all she'll be past child-bearing—'

'Plenty of time for that, surely?' said Owen.

'Well, yes, you're quite right. In theory. But the years soon go. You know that when you're as old as I am. And you've got to manage more than two. Two only replaces; you've got to do better than that if you want to expand. Four! Four children is what we've got to aim for. At least!'

'Anyone as beautiful as your granddaughter should have no difficulty.'

'Oh, there's plenty of men who want to marry her. That's not the problem. The difficulty is on her side. She won't have them. Mind you,' the old man conceded, 'I can't say I blame her. A spineless lot! No spirit! I've been looking at younger ones,' he said, 'the fifteen-year-olds, but it's hard to tell at that age. They're all so well behaved! Maybe one of them—'

'For heaven's sake, Grandfather!' said the girl, coming back with the coffee. 'Do we have to bore the Mamur Zapt with our intimate details?'

'She's quite right!' said the old man. 'She's right again. You ought to have been a boy, Katarina; in fact, you ought to have been your father. A nice, gentle, loving man, but he hasn't got your spirit!'

'Grandfather! There you go again!'

'She's right! I'm getting too old, that's the trouble. I must concentrate. Now, about these soldiers—'

'Again, I must apologize.'

'Well, men must be men, I suppose. If they were not, where would we be? Better that than the reverse. There are too many youngsters these days—'

'Grandfather!' said Katarina warningly.

'Yes, well, as I was saying, men must be men. They were soldiers, after all. I was a soldier once—'

There was a faint sigh from Katarina.

'Not only that,' said Owen quickly, 'the fighting started, or so I understand, over a question of honour. National honour.'

'Really?' said the old man.

'Yes. Some of these soldiers are Welsh. That is to say, they come from the *Pays de Galles*. It's part of Britain, a separate country, you understand, only we were taken over by England—'

'A separate country? Taken over?'

'A long time ago, of course. A very long time ago. Centuries.'

'You said "we".'

'Well, I have to confess, I'm Welsh myself.'

'You are? Well, that is most interesting. Most, in fact, encouraging. And these soldiers were Welsh?'

'Half of them. Something stupid was said, whether it was by the Welsh or by the English, I don't know, but exception was taken to the remark—they were looking for a fight, anyway, I imagine—and then the stupid idiots—'

'Not stupid at all! Quite proper. One must defend one's nation's honour. And some of these were Welsh you say?'

'Yes—'

'There are mountains in Wales? I heard them singing of valleys and where there are valleys there must be—'

'Hills, rather. Yes, the Welsh are very attached to their valleys.'

'A mountaineering race?'

'Well, no, I wouldn't go so far as to say that.'

'You are too modest. Mountaineers *and* fighting men!'

'Look, Wales is not exactly like the Caucasus—'

'Too modest, too modest! But then, you don't have to assert yourselves like us. We are only a small country.'

'Wales, actually, is not that large.'

'A small country too!' The old man almost rubbed his hands. 'Then there are affinities between us. Language? Now what is your language?'

'Welsh. Look—'

'A separate language? Distinct?'

'Yes, but—'

'Threatened?' the old man said significantly.

'Well, yes, there's a danger of it dying out—'

The old man sat back.

'Perhaps this is the answer to our prayers,' he said.

'I don't quite—'

'So many things in common. Perhaps we could stretch a point: Mingrelians and neighbouring countries.'

'Neighbouring? They're about a million miles apart.'

'I was talking spiritually. Neighbouring in spirit. It's reasonable. Sometimes we used to go out and capture a woman from a neighbouring tribe and there was never any difficulty about that. She soon became assimilated. Of course, that was a man taking a woman. It would be different if it was a woman taking a man. Of course, times are different now. More liberated. I see no reason why a woman shouldn't take a husband from a neighbouring tribe, neighbouring spiritually, I mean—'

'Grandfather!' said Katarina, scandalized. She took him by the arm. 'Come on!' she said. 'It's time you went up for your nap!'

'Yes, yes.' He stood up shakily. Owen realized that he was far older than he appeared. 'I accept your apology,' he said suddenly.

'Thank you. I can only repeat—'

'But I'm not withdrawing the complaint.'

'Not withdrawing the complaint? But—'

'We have to stand up for ourselves. Even against our friends. We must not back down.'

'But surely an apology—'

'No. I feel half inclined, I must say, to accept it from the Welsh but not from the English, but that would hardly be fair. Anyway, what does it matter? What is a complaint? In Egypt?'

'Well, we don't like to leave complaints unanswered—'

'Think nothing of it. Now that you have apologized, we shall not take military action.'

'Thank you. But couldn't you withdraw your complaint as well? The fact is, well, there was another complaint too, and it's a bit awkward—'

'Another complaint?'

'Yes, from the Russian Chargé, actually, and we're a bit afraid there might be international—'

'Russian? Did you say Russian? The soldiers insulted him as well?'

'Well, yes, I'm afraid so—'

'Brave men! Magnificent men! There, what did I tell you?' he said fiercely, snatching his arm from Katarina's hold. 'Men of spirit! God, that's the way to treat the Russians! Our allies! Didn't I tell you they were our natural allies? God, if only I was young again—'

Katarina dragged him towards the door.

'Complaint?' he shouted over his shoulder. 'No complaint at all. Far from it! The Russians? Oh, no complaint at all!'

Chapter 3

'It's an affront!' said the Chargé.

'Which we deeply regret,' said Paul, 'and shall do something about.'

'Have already done something about,' supplemented Owen. Paul had asked for support in his grovel and Owen had agreed to accompany him.

'I am glad to hear it,' said the Chargé. 'The men have been flogged?'

'Well, not exactly—'

'Yet,' said Owen quickly. 'There are a few processes to go through first.'

'A military court, you mean? Well, there is something to be said for letting criminals experience the full majesty of the law. It inculcates respect for authority.'

'Quite so.'

'All the same,' said the Chargé, 'the sooner they are flogged, the better. It's like a dog. The longer the gap between crime and punishment the harder it is for the creature to understand. Soldiers are animals and should be treated as such.'

'Well, yes, but—'

'Believe me. I was in the Army myself, the Russian Army, that is. I know. They're all peasants, you see, and as stupid as oxes. The only way you can drive anything into their thick heads is with the whip. Even then it's difficult. Being peasants, they're used to it. They don't feel it as we would. It's got to follow sharply after the event. And no half measures, either! How many lashes?'

'How many—?'

'I'd advise at least sixty. Some say forty, but I think you've got to allow for the sun—'

'The *sun?*'

'Hardens the skin. They don't feel it as much. No, in my view sixty should be standard. Of course, in a case as serious as this the standard is hardly good enough. No, on second thoughts it should be more. Eighty, perhaps. A hundred for the ringleaders.'

'We'll bear your advice in mind.'

'Do. Do. Glad to share my experience with you. You'll let them drink, of course?'

'Well, I rather think they've been doing too much of that already—'

'No, no. Just before they're flogged. A glass or two of vodka. It makes it easier for them. I used to give them a bottle. I'm a humane man, you know.'

'Well, of course, each country has its own practices—'

'It doesn't have to be vodka. Whisky would do. Or rum. You used to use rum, I believe, in the British Navy?'

'I believe so, yes. A while ago.'

'It's better if they're drunk. Mind you, some would say they're drunk all the time.'

'Yes, our soldiers have much in common.'

'Discipline. That's what they need.'

'They certainly do. And I'm sorry you should have suffered because of a lack of it on the part of our soldiers.'

'It's nothing, it's nothing. If it were just myself I would say no more. But, of course, an affront to my country—well, I am bound to resist that. Especially with the Grand Duke's visit so imminent.'

'Grand Duke?' said Owen.

'Yes. Only two and a half weeks away. I tick off each day on my calendar. Between you and me, it will be a great relief when it's all over. If anything goes wrong, it'll be my head on the block. Not literally, of course. We're not a barbarous people.'

'I must apologize once again,' said Paul, beginning to rise from his chair.

'Say no more about it. A mere bagatelle. A few drunken muzhiks, that's all it was. Of course, I cannot formally withdraw my complaint.'

'Oh, dear,' said Paul, sitting down again. 'I was hoping—'

'If it was me, that would be the end of it. But, of course, when it's my country—'

'No insult was *intended*, Chargé!'

'Of course not. They were too drunk to know what they were doing. But one was *received*, and since it was in public, and in view of the forthcoming visit—'

'But, Chargé, precisely because of the forthcoming visit, mightn't we hush things up? We don't want a diplomatic incident, do we?'

'*We* don't,' said the Chargé, 'but back at home *they* might.'

'I must confess this is a blow, Chargé. I had hoped for a quiet run-up to the Grand Duke's visit.'

'Me too,' said the Chargé.

'You don't think you could postpone your complaint? Say, till after the visit was over?'

'It's already with the Parquet. It wouldn't look good if I was to withdraw it and then put it back in.'

'True, true. All the same—the fact is, Chargé, this stupid incident comes at a most awkward time.'

'I can see that. Any other time, the British wouldn't pay any attention.'

'Well, that's exactly it. Go on, Chargé, be a decent chap and I will send you round a bottle of Château d'Yquem.'

'Well—' said the Chargé, weakening.

'You're the only one who's left now.'

'There were others? Other countries are involved?'

'No, no! It's just that the Mingrelian community—'

'Mingrelian!' The Chargé shot upright. 'They were behind it?'

'No, no! They were on the receiving end, actually—'

'Assaulted?'

'I'm afraid so.'

The Chargé leaped up from his chair and threw his arms around Paul.

'The Mingrelians? Assaulted? But this is excellent news, excellent!' He folded Owen, too, in a deep embrace. 'My government will be delighted! Oh, that's the way to do it! First we give it them back at home, now you give it them here! Excellent!'

He pressed the bell on his desk.

'Vodka!' he shouted. 'Vodka, to celebrate! A toast! Undying friendship between our countries!' He pressed Paul emotionally to him once again. 'That is the way allies should behave! I will let my people know at once. The Mingrelians! Thrashed! And that's even before Duke Nicholas gets here—'

He stopped suddenly.

'Why not?' he said. 'Why not? I'll put it to him. Those fine, brave men! A medal! For service to the Tsar! I'll do it! You can rely on me!'

'And the complaint? You withdraw the complaint?'

'Complaint?' said the Chargé. 'What complaint? I have no complaint. Oh, no! Far from it!'

ᔕᔕᔕ

'The Grand Duke's visit?' said Owen.

'I was going to tell you about it. It's just that I didn't want to bother you when your mind was on more important things, like the cafés. The Khedive has invited him. In about three weeks' time.'

'A State Visit?'

'Semi-State. Duke Nicholas is only the heir. He's supposed
to be on an informal tour of the Mediterranean. Well, actually,
he's so unpopular at home that the Tsar wanted to get him
out of the country before someone threw a bomb at him.'

'And the Khedive invited him *here*?'

'That's right. You, of course, will be responsible for security.'

ᏻᏽᎧ

'There's going to be a ball,' said Zeinab.

'It's not been decided yet.'

'And that, of course,' said Zeinab, disregarding him,
'creates a major problem: what am I going to wear?'

'It's not been decided yet. The meeting's not till tomorrow.
Look, I know. I'm going to it.'

'And then there will be the opera as well. I'll need two
dresses. The trouble is, there isn't a decent dress in Cairo.
Anton says he might be getting some in, but everyone will
be fighting for them and, besides, they'll all have seen them.
So I thought I would cable Paris direct. Now here's the
problem: I don't want to do it through Posts and Telegraphs
in the ordinary way, or else people will get to know about it.
So—look, are you listening, this is important—can you send
a cable for me? Using the diplomatic channel?'

'No. Absolutely not.'

'I'll bet the Consul-General's wife is.'

'What she does is her own business.'

'You don't love me,' said Zeinab.

'Of course I love you. Now—'

'You don't love me. Not in the way he loves her.'

'I should bloody hope not,' said Owen, an image of the
Consul-General and his stately lady coming vividly before
his mind.

'I know what it is. You don't want me to go. You are
ashamed of me. There will be all those lords and ladies, those
petty princelings from petty little countries, Wales, I wouldn't
be surprised, and you say: what is an Egyptian woman doing

among that lot? Well, let me tell you, the daughter of a Pasha, *especially* the illegitimate daughter of a Pasha, has got more love and life and passion in her little finger than any of them have in their whole body!'

'I think that's more than likely,' said Owen.

'Wasted!' said Zeinab dramatically. 'On you!'

'Not wasted; I greatly enjoy it.'

'In private, yes, but not in public.'

'Well, what the hell do you want us to do? Make love in the middle of Abdin Square?'

'Take me to the ball.'

'I *am* taking you to the ball. If there is one.'

'You know I can't come if I'm not properly dressed.'

'You *will* be properly dressed. You've got lots of dresses. They're all there on the rack. Look, bloody hundreds of them—'

'You want to see me in rags!'

'Rags! This one cost more than a year's pay! You told me. Afterwards.'

'I passed the bill to my father. He will not want to see me dressed like some parvenue. He has pride. We are like that in Egypt. Proud people. We know what is fitting. Unlike the boring, bourgeois British.'

'Look, I am *not* going to use the Diplomatic Postbag just to send a cable to your couturier.'

'Just?' said Zeinab.

☙

Even the flies in the committee room seemed stupefied by the heat. This was unusual, thought Owen, since flies were normally the most active part of the population. Perhaps it was not the heat that was getting to them but committee life. The shutters of the committee room were kept closed in a vain attempt to keep the temperature down and perhaps the flies could never get out. They spent their lives in eternal committee. My God, thought Owen; what a life! For a second or two he felt quite indignant on their behalf but then the heat had its effect on him, too, and he settled back gloomily in his chair.

'The itinerary first,' said Paul. 'Duke Nicholas will transfer to the Khedivial Yacht at Alexandria, pass through the Canal to Suez and then take the overland train to Cairo. He will spend three days in Cairo as the guest of His Royal Highness, the Khedive, and then go upriver to Luxor to view the antiquities. He will then return to Cairo and spend two days at the Palace recovering from the rigours of his journey. Then he will travel by train to Alexandria, spend a day there and depart by boat on the Thursday evening. The whole visit will last twelve days, including the two to be spent on the Royal Yacht.'

'That bit should be all right from the point of view of security,' observed the major.

'He'll be spending a good time on the water, what with the river trip,' said McPhee.

'I'll turn to security later,' said Paul. 'The first question, though, is what we're going to do with him while he's here. The Khedive would like to reproduce as far as possible the visit of Duke Nicholas's uncle, the Crown Prince, when he came here to open the Suez Canal.'

'Out of the question!' said Finance Department immediately. 'Cost too much!'

'"As far as possible",' said Paul. 'Those are the key words, I think. Surely we can accede to His Royal Highness's wishes to that extent? Of course, we may not be able to go as far as he would like—'

'As long as we bear in mind budgetary constraints,' said Finance Department.

'Just so. Now, Mr. Abd-es-Salem is here representing the Court, and I wonder if he could tell us what His Royal Highness has in mind with respect to the programme?'

'Well, last time the Khedive commissioned an opera—'

'No!' said Finance Department quickly.

'—and built the new Opera House.'

'My God!' said Finance Department.

'After consideration, the Khedive would not, perhaps, wish to go so far this time. But he does feel that, in view of its centrality on the previous visit, opera should have at least some part in the programme—'

'Does he now?' said Paul, sitting up.

'Out of the question!' said Finance Department. 'Too costly!'

'Oh, come!'

'That was what bankrupted Egypt in the first place,' said Finance Department.

'What better thing to be bankrupted by?' murmured Paul.

'Actually, I must support the Khedive,' said Owen, who thought there was a chance of getting a performance of *Aida* out of this. 'I feel that since His Royal Highness has expressed the wish to reproduce as closely as possible the original arrangements, we ought to do the best we can to oblige him.'

Mr. Abd-es-Salem flashed him a grateful glance.

'If you're thinking of *Aida*,' said Finance Department smugly, 'you can think again. *Aida* wasn't actually performed on the original visit. It was commissioned for the opening of the Canal but wasn't ready on time. It was performed some time after.'

'All the more reason for the Grand Duke to be able to see it now,' suggested Paul.

'*Aida is completely out of the question*,' said Finance Department with emphasis. 'I have this straight from the Treasury in London.'

'They actually specified there was to be no *Aida*?'

'Certainly. Opera is something they really know about in the Treasury.'

'We could dispense with the animals,' said Paul temptingly.

'Animals?' said the major.

'Live animals were a feature of the original production,' said Finance Department. 'Lots of them! Actually, it wouldn't be a good idea,' he said to Paul. 'Suppose the Grand Duke got eaten?'

'We could keep him away from them. Owen could see to that—'

'No animals,' said Finance Department firmly. 'And no *Aida*, either. Of course, there is no reason why you shouldn't choose another opera. The Treasury is not opposed to opera in principle. Far from it.'

'Well, that *is* a helpful suggestion,' said Paul. 'Now—'

The Army had been fidgeting for some time.

'Could we get on to the real business?'

Paul raised his eyebrows.

'I thought that was the real business,' he said.

'What about security?'

'We've got to agree on the programme first, haven't we? Right, let's move on. There will be a Grand Ball, of course …'

'There could be difficulties,' said Owen.

'What difficulties?'

'Well, dresses. That kind of thing.'

Paul glanced at his notes.

'No, this has already been decided. The Consul-General's wife—'

⌒⟳

'A March Past?' suggested the Army, some time later.

'March Past?'

'The Khedive reviewing his troops.'

'There may be international observers,' said Paul. 'I don't think we should make our military presence too obvious. We could have a jolly procession, I suppose.'

'The Khedive would like that,' said Mr. Abd-es-Salem. 'In fact, he would wish to take part in it himself. He could ride at the head with the Grand Duke in an open landau.'

'Is that a good idea?' asked Owen.

'Why not?' said Mr. Abd-es-Salem, surprised.

'Because it would make it easy for someone to take a pot shot at him.'

'The Khedive feels safe with his people,' said Mr. Abd-es-Salem reprovingly.

'I was thinking of the Grand Duke,' said Owen hastily and untruly.

'Surely there is no risk of that?'

'Cairo is a city of many nationalities. And not all of them are sympathetic to Russia.'

'Even so—'

'The Balkan countries, for instance.'

'Ah, yes,' said Mr. Abd-es-Salem thoughtfully. 'The Balkans!'

'The Mingrelians!' added Owen, for the benefit of the Army.

'My God, yes!' said the major. 'The Mingrelians!'

'Round them up,' said Shearer. 'Round them all up!'

'All of them?' said Owen. 'There are over twenty thousand people from various Balkan countries in Cairo alone. The place is like a miniature Balkans. It's a potential powder keg, I can tell you. I think this visit is crazy. Why don't we call the whole thing off?'

'Call it off?' said Mr. Abd-es-Salem, aghast. 'His Royal Highness has set his heart on it!'

'I'm afraid we've gone too far down the road to call it off now,' said Paul. 'Although I agree with you about the potential threat.'

'Threat?' said Mr. Abd-es-Salem, with considerable asperity. 'Are you saying that the British can no longer maintain order? Even with an Army?'

'Certainly not!' said the major indignantly.

'We can handle it,' said Captain Shearer.

'Can you?' said Owen quickly. 'Well, there's a lot to be said for—'

'No chance!' said Paul firmly. 'It has already been decided that the Mamur Zapt has overall responsibility for the security arrangements. But a good try!' he added, turning to Owen.

～⁂～

'You again?' said the café owner. He was sitting with his legs heavily bandaged and propped across a chair in front of him.

'I like coffee,' said Owen.

'You don't think you could enjoy it somewhere else?'

'I especially like it here.'

'You get in the way, you know.'

'You mean, the men won't come while I'm here? Isn't that a good thing?'

'I don't know. They'll come again when you're not here.'

'I could leave someone with you.'

'They're big blokes.'

'This is a big bloke.'

'Hanging around all day drinking coffee?'

'He could work for you. In fact, it would be better if he did. You could say he had come up from the country.'

'Why don't you just go away?' said the café owner.

'I'm like the other lot. I'm never going to go away.'

The café owner cursed softly.

'You get me down,' he said. 'You really do.'

'I'm your only way out,' said Owen. 'You'll be glad of me. Later.'

'A lot later,' said the café owner. 'When I'm in heaven.'

'Even before. It's just the next bit that's hard.'

'Why pick the hard way?'

'Because if you pick the other way, it never ends. You don't just pay once. You go on paying. You pay all the time. They come more often. And after a while they ask for more. And then more. And then more still. In the end you're working only for them. All you've built up is theirs. Look, I know what it takes to build up a place like this, what it costs you.

It costs you years of your life and you've only got one life. Going to give it all away, now, are you?'

'I'm not giving anything away,' said the café owner. 'But I'm still thinking.'

'Think on. Take the long view. You've had to take the long view, haven't you, all your life? Otherwise you'd never have got where you are. Think long now. My way is hard at first but then there's an end to it. The other way is easy today and hard tomorrow. And tomorrow goes on for a long time.'

'The only thing is,' said the café owner, 'that I like the idea of there being tomorrows.'

'The man I put in is always there. He sleeps under the table. He doesn't go home at night.' Owen had a sudden pang of conscience. Selim wouldn't care for this bit. 'He never leaves you,' he said, nevertheless, determinedly.

'And he works?'

'A big, strong man.'

'You're not doing this for my sake,' said the café owner.

'Of course not. There are other cafés.'

'Why don't you ask them?'

'I'm asking you. I need someone like you.'

'Stubborn?'

'Greedy,' said Owen. 'Greedy to cling on to his own.'

The café owner laughed.

'Well, you've got the right man,' he said. 'I don't believe in giving money away.'

'When it's hard earned, it's not easily given.'

'That, too, is true,' said the man. 'Well. I'll think about it.'

'While you're thinking,' said Owen, 'I could be doing something. If you would just give me a start.'

'What is it you want to know?'

'The name.'

The gangs usually left their name. It was normal, for example, to sign extortion notes. Not that the name in itself meant much. Arab taste for the lurid produced such names as 'The Red Sword', 'Hand of Blood' or 'The Red Eye'; but the readiness of the groups to give their names made it easy to ascribe activities to the group and Nikos now had a file on most of them.

The name would probably be enough to tell Owen what kind of gang he was dealing with. He would probably be able to tell, for example, whether the gang was a straight-forward criminal one or whether it was a terrorist one arising out of a political club.

Cairo seethed with political discussion, most of which took place openly in the cafés. You could have a good argument any night of the week almost anywhere. Some of it, however, took place privately in clubs specially formed for the purpose. These still met in cafés—that was what Cairo cafés were for!—but now it was in an inner room where members could more properly indulge their taste for the melodramatic. There were dozens of such clubs in Cairo and no dashing young effendi could afford to admit that he had never been to one.

Most of the clubs were heavily Nationalist and some were revolutionary. Of these, a small minority was committed to violent action now and sought to finance their activities by engaging in the protection racket.

'I don't know their name,' said the café owner.

'It would help me a lot. It could help you a lot.'

'Help me to get my neck broken. No thanks.'

ᘓᴥᴥᴥᕽ

Another café, later. This was the life, Owen decided. It had always been a desire of his to obliterate completely the line between work and play, so that work would seem like play and play would carry the moral justification of work. In Cairo, where business was habitually transacted in cafés, that was easy. You had to meet a colleague? Where better than in a café? Offices were hot and hard edged, uncongenial to the Arab, who liked to pour the syrup of emotion over everything. They lacked conviviality, whereas to the Arab, conviviality was all.

At the table next to him two men stood up, shook hands, picked up their decorated leather briefcases and left. They had been discussing a contract for the delivery of sesame. The man remaining turned immediately, greeted some acquaintance at another table, pulled his chair across and lunged into an animated discussion of the merits of some Ghawazee singers at a place near the Clot Bey. So easily did business turn to pleasure. So, too, did it turn to politics. At the table on his other side some young effendi were arguing hotly about Egypt's place in the world, asking why cultural importance, as evinced by the constant flood of tourists, was not reflected in political significance.

Across the tables he suddenly caught sight of Mahmoud and waved an arm. Mahmoud, however, had already seen him and was weaving his way through the tables to join him.

'A relief!' he said, dropping into a chair. 'I was in court all morning. And then some papers I need for tomorrow hadn't arrived so I spent the afternoon chasing them. And then when they did arrive they weren't what I wanted, so I had to start all over again. I've only just got away!'

No other lawyer, Owen suspected, whether Egyptian or British, would work through the heat of the Egyptian afternoon. Mahmoud, however, was a perfectionist and couldn't imagine going into court unless he was absolutely sure of his ground; and absolutely meant absolutely. They talked for a while about the case Mahmoud was engaged on and then Mahmoud asked him what he was busy with.

Owen told him about the protection racket.

'Cafés, now, is it?' said Mahmoud. He knew, of course, about the gangs. If Owen's work reached the stage of prosecution, it would be the Parquet who would handle it.

Owen nodded.

'A new target. Rather a tempting one,' he said, looking around. 'Fat pickings.'

'Political?' asked Mahmoud. He knew about the clubs, too. Indeed, he almost certainly went to one himself.

'I don't know. I wish I could find out.'

'From my point of view it doesn't matter much. Crime is crime.'

'It matters to me. If they're doing it for money, it ends there. If they're doing it for political reasons, you ask what it's going to issue in later. Bombs?'

'You think this new burst of activity might be related to some particular issue that they have in mind?'

'I'm wondering.'

Mahmoud, interested, sat thinking.

'Yes,' he said, 'I can see it makes a difference to you. That is because you are always thinking about prevention. Well, that is good. Forestalling violence must always be good. So long as you yourself keep within the law. The law must always be supreme. Even expediency, which is, of course, the justification you can always cite, must bow to the law. Otherwise there is injustice, and that is a worse crime than violence, for violence is merely a fault of the individual, whereas injustice is a fault in the society.'

Mahmoud was a great legalist. He believed passionately in the law, which, of course, left him in rather an isolated position in Egypt. It even created difficulties for him as a Nationalist because, while it was easy enough to oppose the illegal British and the corrupt regime of the Pashas which had preceded it, he also opposed extra-legal action, such as violence. Peaceful demonstrations, he believed in; but then, as Owen frequently said to him (they spent many happy hours in cafés arguing the point), what demonstration in Egypt ever stayed peaceful?

'Everyone is subject to the law,' repeated Mahmoud stubbornly. 'Even the British,' he said sternly.

It gave Owen an opportunity.

'About those complaints …' he said.

'Complaints?'

'Those bloody fools in the café the other night.'

'There was more than one complaint?'

'Oh, yes. Not that it matters, now that they've both been withdrawn.'

'Withdrawn? I didn't know that the complaint had been withdrawn.'

'Oh, yes.'

'Have you been leaning on them?' said Mahmoud, his cheeks beginning to tauten.

'I wouldn't say leaning; it was more confused than that.'

He wondered whether he should tell Mahmoud about the two conversations.

'Anyway, it is prejudicing the inquiry,' said Mahmoud. 'And that is interfering with the cause of justice.'

'These people were pretty prejudiced already.'

Mahmoud was silent. He was used, of course, to this kind of situation. But it made him angry.

'The investigation continues,' he said coldly.

'Even if the originating complaint is withdrawn?'

'It's on the files now. Besides, we don't need a complaint. We can proceed without it. It was a clear breach of public order.'

'No one's denying that. It's just a question of what's the appropriate action. Is it a matter for the civil courts? Or for the military ones?'

This was a mistake, for Mahmoud knew a lot more about the law than he did.

'Both,' said Mahmoud. 'However, what the Army does is no concern of mine. I do not have any say in it. Nor do I expect the Army to have any say in whether there is a civil prosecution or not.'

'Not "say",' said Owen. '"Request", more like. The Army requests the Parquet to leave the action in this case to its authorities.'

'Well, if it cares to put in a formal request…I shall oppose it, though the decision, in the end, will not be up to me. It will go to the Minister. And I daresay,' said Mahmoud bitterly, 'if you are wondering, that your Legal Adviser will be able to persuade the Minister, as usual, that it is not in his interests to allow the matter to proceed. But I,' he added furiously, 'shall lodge a complaint.'

'That's four,' said Owen.

'Four?' said Mahmoud, startled.

'One from you; one from Shearer—that's that difficult Army captain; one from the Mingrelians, and one from the Russian Chargé.'

'Is he in it?'

'He was in it. Now he's withdrawn. In view of the Grand Duke's visit,' he explained, thinking this might mollify Mahmoud.

'Grand Duke?' said Mahmoud.

Owen told him what he knew about Duke Nicholas's visit. Mahmoud shrugged his shoulders.

'Excuse me,' said one of the young effendi at the next table, 'but I couldn't help overhearing: this visit of the Russian Duke, what is its nature?'

'Well, I gather the Khedive hopes to replicate an earlier visit, when the Duke's uncle came to open the Suez Canal.'

'Would you say it was cultural in purpose? Or political?'

'Bit of both, I suppose. But cultural, mainly.'

'There you are!' The young man turned back triumphantly to his colleagues. 'Cultural recognition leads to political recognition!'

'What the earlier visit led to,' said one of the young man's colleagues, 'was bankruptcy. And *that* led to the British taking over.'

Chapter 4

'Oh, no!' said the café owner.

'But yes!' said Owen brightly, looking around for a place to sit and finally choosing one right next to where the owner was sprawled against a table, bandaged legs stretching over a chair in front of him. 'I like your coffee!'

'Mekhmet!'

A small, frightened-looking man scuttled in.

'Mekhmet, some coffee for our guest!'

'Right, Sidi Mustapha!' said the man, touching his brow. 'At once!'

He made for the door.

'And put some poison in it!' shouted the owner.

The little man stopped in the doorway, confused.

'Go on, you fool! It's only a joke.'

He clapped his hands impatiently.

The little man's eyes rolled, panic-stricken.

'Oh, my God!' said the owner. 'Get on with it, you fool. Get some coffee!'

A woman stuck her head out of a door at the back.

'Don't shout at him!' she said indignantly. 'He's a poor, afflicted creature! He's doing his best!'

'He's not doing anything at all!' shouted the café owner. 'He's just standing there!'

'You've confused him! Come on, Mekhmet, love,' she said kindly. 'Take no notice of him!'

The owner groaned and put a fist to his head.

'It's impossible!' he said. 'The man's a halfwit. Tell him anything and he gets confused. You can't run a café business like that! I'm only employing him because he's her sister-in-law's cousin.'

The woman emerged from the back with some coffee for Owen.

'You're only employing him because he's cheap!' she said tartly. 'You thought you could get something for nothing.'

'I was wrong, then, wasn't I? I haven't even got something!'

'You're a hard-hearted man,' she said. 'If you turn your face from God's poor, He will turn his face from you!'

'You get back inside, woman!' shouted Mustapha indignantly. 'Showing yourself off in public to all the men!'

'If you're going to shout at Mekhmet when he brings the coffee, and you're going to shout at me, who's going to bring it, I'd like to know? You just tell me that!'

She stalked off. The café owner mopped his brow.

'Just look at that!' he said. 'Women are all the same. Difficult! She wouldn't have married me if it hadn't been for the dowry. Now she expects me to provide for everybody! Anyone who's simple or lame or blind she invites in. Turn my face from God's poor? I'm going to *be* one of God's poor if she carries on the way she's going.'

'The fact is, you need a man about the place,' said Owen.

Mustapha looked at him.

'You on that again?'

'It's the answer to your prayers.'

Mustapha was silent for some time.

'Is he smart?' he said at last.

'He's big,' said Owen.

The café owner chuckled.

'Like that, is it? Well, it's not altogether a bad thing. Get somebody smart and the next thing you know, they've got something going on the side. Big and willing, that's all you want. At least, that's what the farmers used to say back in the village when I was a boy. And—he's not going to cost anything?'

'Even less than Mekhmet,' said Owen.

ᏀᎲᎲᎥᎲ

The Grand Duke's visit had been announced the day before and the newspapers were full of it. The tone was broadly welcoming. Even the Nationalist papers—and most of the papers were Nationalist—took a positive view of the visit as a mark of international recognition.

There were, of course, as always in Cairo, exceptions. For the most part these were confined to the Balkan communities and Owen realized now for the first time how many of these there were in the city. He had been hazily aware, for example, of the Montenegrins parading in their big boots outside the chief hotels for the benefit of tourists, but had not realized until now that they formed a substantial community. He had vaguely registered that Serbs were always fighting Croats and Bosnians Herzegovinians, but since in Egypt at any rate they were prudently not fighting Muslims he had taken this as merely the expression of an over-exuberant national spirit and left it to the ordinary police. Lots of them though there were, there had not been enough for him to register them as a significant political presence. Up till now.

Each community, it soon transpired, was holding a public meeting to protest against Duke Nicholas's visit. Indeed, some of them were cooperating in holding joint meetings so things must be really serious. Since the meetings were all obligingly announced in the press, Owen assumed at first that he had little to worry about.

'It's not public meetings that lead to assassinations,' he said to Paul, when the Consul-General registered alarm at the vehemence of some of the meetings, 'but private ones.'

'What a decent British thing to say!' said Paul. 'I only hope that you are right.'

However, he took the precaution of posting observers at all the meetings, whereupon he found that *all* the meetings were plotting the Grand Duke's assassination. He was much perturbed and started following developments very closely; until he found that the exuberance of spirit that he had detected earlier worked against agreement on specific proposals. He continued to follow developments but sat back and relaxed until one morning Nikos brought him news of yet another protest meeting scheduled for the following evening in Old Cairo.

'Babylon?' said Owen, surprised. 'I didn't think there were any of them there. I thought it was only Copts and Greeks.'

'And a few others,' said Nikos, who was himself a Copt and viewed all other races as interlopers.

Babylon, as Old Cairo was confusingly known, was situated about three miles south of the modern city. It was built on the site of the old Roman fortress, very little of which now remained. The scanty ruins of the walls had been largely incorporated into the Coptic Ders. A peculiarity of the area was that many of the Coptic and Greek churches had been built within walled enclosures known as Ders. These usually contained shops and schools and houses as well as churches so that they took on the character of fortified precincts.

It was in one of these Ders, or precincts, that the meeting was to be held. Like most public meetings in Cairo it was held in the open air, in a small square at the heart of the enclosure. When Owen arrived, the square was already comfortably filled. Most people were in ordinary Arab dress, tending towards the black and grey of the Copt rather than the blue and white or striped of the ordinary Egyptian fellahin. Owen was surprised. The Copts had survived for centuries by keeping their heads down. What now was bringing them out in protest? Surely not a Russian Grand Duke?

As he continued to look, however, he saw that most of them were not actually Copts, but he could not make out what they were. Some of them wore crosses, so they were Christians, but their features were not those of Copts. Copts' faces were round; these were aquiline. Some of them wore boots, too, the high-heeled boots of the Montenegrins; and some were in breeches. He wondered who they could be.

At one end of the square was a raised platform for the speakers and now the speakers were coming out. They filed across the stage and sat down on the chairs provided. Behind them a huge banner was suddenly unfolded. It said, in great fiery letters: 'Death to the Grand Duke!' Which was not very promising.

A man stood up and began to address the meeting, in Arabic. He said that the meeting had been called in order to allow people to express their views on the subject of the forthcoming visit of the Grand Duke and decide what action, if any, should be taken. He then began to call on the speakers.

One after another they came forward and spoke of what the Russians had done. If half of what they said was true, thought Owen, they had every reason to feel bitter. God, it was terrible! Each one recited a litany of atrocities.

It took him quite a while to work out where each speaker was from. Armenia, yes, that was fairly clear, and Georgia— there seemed a lot of Georgians about, judging by the applause. Azerbaijan, well, yes, just about; but Dagestan? Dagestan! And Abkhaz? Where the hell was Abkhaz? What the hell was Abkhaz, come to that!

And now someone else was coming forward, someone who seemed vaguely familiar—God, it was Sorgos!

He stood for a moment looking down at the crowd. He had discarded his stick and looked years younger. A torch nearby lit up the sharp face and the thin bony hands clutching the edges of the rostrum. He seemed like some great eagle standing there. He now raised one of the hands.

'The task,' he said, 'is not to complain about what has been done to us; but to avenge it!'

The whole front of the crowd jumped to its feet and began applauding vigorously. For several minutes Sorgos was unable to speak. Then he raised his hand again. The noise died away.

'I had a house once,' he said. 'I had a family, I had a village. And I prayed that the Russians would not come and visit it. But one day they did. And then I had a different prayer. It was that they would come again. Only this time I would be waiting. And I would know what to do!'

He paused for a moment, breathing heavily. His audience was silent, gripped.

'And now my prayer has been answered,' he said quietly. 'The Russian is coming; and I know what to do.'

The strength seemed suddenly to leave his body. He turned away from the rostrum. Friends rushed forward to help him back to his seat.

But meanwhile the crowd had erupted. Everyone was on their feet shouting and waving. There was pandemonium. The front of the crowd surged forwards. Others pushed in behind them. And now, looking round, Owen saw that the square was packed and everywhere, in the torchlight, faces were contorted and crying. Over to one side some men were trying to climb on to the platform and beside them a man in boots had scrambled up some scaffolding and was half turned towards the crowd, shaking his fist and screaming.

And then Owen lost sight of the platform altogether as the crowd around him eddied forward and took him with them and he had to concentrate on keeping his footing.

The man who had opened the meeting was standing up at the rostrum and pleading with the crowd to keep order. Others on the platform had got out of their seats and come forward to the edge from where they were trying to shout to their supporters. There were stewards, but they were helpless as the crowd swirled to and fro about them.

In a way it was fortunate both that the square was small and that the crowd was now so tightly packed as to make it hard to fall. Owen was trying to fight his way forward to the platform but everyone else was trying to do the same. He was afraid that at any moment someone would go down and then within seconds it would be frightful. He levered himself up on someone's shoulder and began to shout commands; one or two faces turned towards him but in the uproar most of his words were lost.

And then suddenly, by chance, probably, the tumult died down and the chairman was able to make himself heard. He was a doctor or something and had some presence or at least experience of chairing meetings. Gradually he cajoled the meeting back to order.

'Calm, friends, calm!' he cried. 'Let us resume the meeting! There is work to be done!'

From over to one side, the side where the men had climbed on to the platform, he received sudden support.

'Order! Order! There is work to be done!' bellowed a loud voice.

'Let's get on with it!' shouted someone near him.

The swirls steadied and the noise dropped.

'I call on Mr. Karamajoric!' cried the chairman, and Mr. Karamajoric came forward. The mood of the meeting had changed, however, and no one wanted to listen any more to another litany of grievances. The chairman, realizing this, intervened swiftly and sent Mr. Karamajoric back to his place.

'Before I close the meeting,' he shouted, 'let us agree on what is to be done next. I propose a committee to—'

'A committee?' shouted a voice over on the right. 'What do we need a committee for?'

'There are too many of us. If a few of us could work something out—'

'What is there to work out? We know what to do, don't we?'

'A petition—'

But his words were drowned.

'Death to the Grand Duke!' came the cry.

ᕙᆖᕗ

'A good meeting, wasn't it?' said Sorgos, embracing Owen warmly.

'If someone had died it wouldn't have been a good meeting!'

Sorgos's face clouded over momentarily.

'No one was hurt, were they? The crowd did seem to get a bit out of hand. But that's good, isn't it? You want people to have a bit of life in them. You don't want them to be dull under oppression. You want them to rise up, to rise up—'

'It's all very well rising up over in the Caucasus but this is someone else's country and you can't expect them to let you rise up here.'

'You rise up against oppression,' said Sorgos, 'whether it's there or here. And you rise up against the Russians anywhere you get the chance.'

'The Khedive would see you as a guest. He has very generously allowed you to live here and when he invites other guests he expects you to treat them with the same generosity.'

'You wouldn't treat the Russians with generosity,' said Sorgos; 'not if they'd been to your village in Wales!'

'Those battles are for the Caucasus. We've got enough trouble of our own here without your adding to it.'

'Trouble? What kind of trouble? I have lived here for thirty years and I have not seen any trouble. Not as it is in the Caucasus, anyway. That's *real* trouble! Egypt is a peaceful country. Except when your soldiers go out and wreck a café. Just exuberance, of course,' he added conciliatorily.

'Trouble between Muslim and Christian,' said Owen sternly. 'That's what I'm worried about.'

'No problem,' Sorgos assured him. 'This is strictly between Christian and Christian.'

'Yes. But it wouldn't stay that way. Not in Cairo.'

'They would take our side? Well, that is understandable. They are men of spirit. Fine men! I know them. We fought side by side against the Russians.'

'Wait a minute; where is this?'

'Back home in the Caucasus. The Muslims were our allies. Against the Russians. I won't pretend we always saw eye to eye. There were differences between us. I mean, we had been fighting each other for several centuries. The Muslims were our natural enemy, you might say. But then the Russians came along and they were even more our natural enemy, so we sank our differences and fought side by side. Fine men! And women, too. To tell you the truth'—Sorgos drew Owen to him and whispered in his ear—'I think Katarina has got a bit of Muslim blood in her. It was always claimed that her grandmother's father had taken a girl from one of the tribes. A raid, you know. There were plenty in those days. And I think it was sometimes done for the sake of the women—'

Owen piloted him gently out of the square. The old man was still buoyant with excitement and Owen knew that his words were getting nowhere. He would have to talk with him again tomorrow. And with the others. The old man was in many respects the key, however. He seemed to have a bit of a following and they couldn't all be Mingrelians, either, if what Katarina had said was true, that there were only sixty families left. Perhaps the fact that he was an elder was something to do with it. He was looked to generally for leadership. Or, perhaps, of course, he was being used.

A man came running out of the square after them. He came up to them and threw his arms around Sorgos.

'I wanted to catch you before you left,' he said. 'A wonderful speech! The fire! That's what was missing until you spoke. I was in despair. And then you came forward—'

'I spoke as a man should.'

'They don't speak like that nowadays.'

'Then they should!'

'Oh, yes,' said the man; 'they should!'

He saw that Owen was supporting the old man and looked at him enquiringly.

'Are you all right?' he asked. 'I'd come with you myself, only—'

'I'll see him home,' said Owen.

The man shook hands with them both and dashed off back into the square. Owen saw that beneath his galabeeyah he was wearing boots.

'A Mingrelian?' he asked.

'Mingrelian?' said Sorgos, surprised. 'No, Georgian.'

He seemed suddenly very tired. The excitement had ebbed. He was barely able to stumble along. Owen offered him an arm, which he accepted gratefully. 'Like a son,' he murmured. 'Like a son.'

He recovered briefly when they reached his house.

'Like a son!' he roared, as Katarina came running to the door.

'What?' said Katarina.

'He's been like a son to me,' said Sorgos, gesturing in Owen's direction.

'Well, that's nice,' said Katarina.

'I needed a bit of help to get home.'

'I told you you would,' said Katarina, annoyed. 'But you wouldn't listen.'

'There was work to be done. Work for men.'

'You leave it to the men, then. You've had your turn. Just help me a moment, would you?' she said to Owen.

Together they got Sorgos to a divan. Katarina lifted his legs up and gently pushed him back. He fell asleep immediately.

'He's going to overdo it one of these days,' she said.

'He's overdone it tonight,' said Owen.

'What's he been saying?'

'It isn't the saying,' said Owen. 'It's what might follow on from the saying.'

'It's only words now,' said Katarina reassuringly. 'He won't be able to do anything.'

'Only words?' said Owen. 'In a situation like this, words are enough.'

'What is the situation?'

Owen told her.

She was silent for a moment. Then she said: 'He shouldn't come.'

'Duke Nicholas?'

'Duke Nicholas or any other Russian. He's only doing it to provoke us.'

'The Mingrelians? For God's sake, he's probably never heard of the Mingrelians.'

'That may well be true. It's easier to crush a people if you've never heard of them. He *ought* to have heard of us. We were a people. We had lives.'

'Look, I'm not exactly in favour of him coming—'

'Tell me,' she said; 'suppose you are right, and suppose he has never heard of the Mingrelians; and now suppose you tell him they are here, in Cairo, these people whom he crushed. What do you think he will say? Do you think he will be ashamed, do you think he will postpone his visit? I don't think so. I think he will say, let the visit go on. What do we care for these Mingrelians? If they cause trouble, put them down! That is what he will say, won't he?'

'Something like it,' said Owen, remembering the Chargé.

'Very well, then. In that case I am with my grandfather. I think we should stand up. To show that we cannot be put down. We can be knocked down but we will never stay down.'

'Well, I have some sympathy with that,' said Owen. 'But standing up is one thing and throwing a bomb is another.'

'The Russians should have thought of that,' said Katarina, 'when they threw the first bomb.'

'That is all in the past.'

'The past is never all in the past. You always carry some of it with you.'

'You can't do it forever. Where do you think we'd have been in Wales if we'd gone on thinking like that?'

Sorgos stirred in his sleep.

'The Welsh,' he said drowsily. 'A mountain people.'

'That's right,' said Owen. 'We'd still be in the bloody hills, that's where!'

⁖

'—and so the dog dropped the sack and ran away,' said the storyteller, 'and all the names were just left lying there in the street. Now, the trouble was that in all the confusion, and what with all the shaking and jolting they had received, they had got mixed up. There were bits of men's names mixed with bits of women's names. Well, they all began crying out. One would shout, "Who am I?" and the other bit would shout, "you're not you, you're me!" So then they all began fighting each other. Well, then the blind man came running along the road and he tripped on the sack and fell right in on top of them—'

'Ho, ho!' said the big man standing in the doorway. 'Very good!'

'Selim!' came a shout from inside.

'Coming!' called the big man. 'You old bastard!' he added sotto voce.

Owen followed him in.

'Not you again!' said the café owner, aghast.

'Me again,' said Owen cheerfully. 'How are things going?'

'Terribly,' said the café owner. 'Your man is useless. He's big, all right, but he's got something missing up top. The trouble is, that's the sort my wife goes for. They've only got to be simpletons for her to feel all soft about them.'

'She'd better not feel too soft about this bloke,' said Owen uneasily.

'That's just what I've told her! Kick the bugger up the backside, I say. That'll get him moving! Only that's what I say about all of them and she doesn't take a blind bit of notice. Here, you idle sod! Fetch some coffee for the effendi! He's your boss, isn't he?' he added more quietly.

Selim came out of the kitchen looking daggers. He put the coffee before Owen, however, with a flourish.

'Brilliant!' whispered Owen. 'You're doing brilliantly.'

'The next time they beat him up,' Selim whispered back. 'I'll join in and help them!'

'Meanwhile, just put up with him. You're doing very well, and this is important.'

'He just sits there all day giving orders,' said Selim. 'He's worse than a sergeant.'

'Yes, well, don't mind him. It won't be for long. It's just a question of waiting.'

'I don't mind waiting,' said Selim. 'Not if I've got my feet up and a pot of coffee in front of me. But this is not like that. The moment I sit down he's on to me.'

'There are worse things. Just keep it up, that's all. Now listen: there's something you can be doing. Try and find out the name of the gang. Talk to the woman.'

Selim gave a broad smile.

'I'll talk to the woman, all right,' he said.

ဝမ္မာ၁

Owen and Zeinab had been to the opera; in fact, were still at the opera, only, as this was the interval, and intervals were somewhat protracted in Egypt, they were going for a walk round the nearby Ezbekiyeh Gardens. 'Gardens' was perhaps a misnomer. In a country where, given water, anything will grow, and gardens were usually a riot of lush tropical vegetation, the Ezbekiyeh remained barren. There were various explanations for this. The most popular was that it was a British plot; or, conversely, testimony to Egyptian incapacity. Whatever the reason, the fact was that it consisted of only a few scrubby trees and some equally scrubby grass, tempting only for fornicating in, which was the reason, no doubt, why the gardens were fenced off with high iron railings and closed after dark.

What made the gardens fun to walk round was not their inside but their outside. As in the English tabloid newspapers, all human life was there: from the chestnut sellers roasting their chestnuts on the gratings which covered the roots of the young trees which surrounded the gardens—and perhaps that's why the trees were scrubby—to the fortunetellers, usually Nubian women, telling fortunes by reading sand spread on a cloth. There were pavement stalls (rags and sweets in promiscuous proximity), pavement restaurants (consisting of large trays with stew in the middle and hunks of bread stuck on nails around the edge), barber shops (the barbers sat on the railings while their customers stood patiently in front of them), hat stands (on the railings), whip stands (ditto), oleographs of Levantine saints (ditto), indecent postcards (ditto and adjacent) and many other treasures. At intervals along the railings were Cleopatra's Needle-like columns, only they consisted either of tarbooshes piled one on top of the other to an implausible height, or of congealed candy densely spotted with flies.

At night, however, such detail was lost. Lamps on the railings threw a mysterious, hazy glow and the flames of the chestnut-sellers' fires created little pockets of moving light and shadow. Owen, impressionable at the best of times and made more so by the music he had just been listening to, loved it.

They came round on to the Sharia el Genaina, where there was music of a different kind: honky-tonk from the questionable cafés which looked across the street to the houses opposite, where the ladies of the night paraded their charms. In one of the cafés some men were singing mournfully.

'Oh, my God!' said Owen.

'What language is it?' asked Zeinab, puzzled.

'Welsh!'

They could see the singers more clearly now. It was, as Owen had already suspected, his friends, the Welsh Fusiliers.

'Why don't they keep those stupid bastards back in barracks?'

'But why?' demanded Zeinab. 'They sing so beautifully!'

'Because they're drunk. And they'll soon be causing trouble.'

'They are singing because they're unhappy,' said Zeinab indignantly. 'Listen to the music. You can hear!'

'Welshmen always go on like that abroad.'

'They are thinking of their homes. It is in the music,' said Zeinab, who was also impressionable and had also just been to the opera. 'They are far from their country and they are very sad. If I was taken away from my country,' declared Zeinab tragically, turning her great eyes on Owen, 'I would sing like that!'

They had with them one of Zeinab's artistic friends, a musician called Rashid.

'What is interesting,' he said, 'is that they are singing in parts. You don't usually get drunken soldiers doing that!'

'There's a bit of a tradition of choral singing in Wales.'

'Is that so? But this is not what I would normally think of as choral singing. It is not church music, surely?'

'Some of it. But also folk song.'

'It is the spirit of the people,' said Zeinab firmly, 'speaking in music.'

'Well—'

'Speaking in music,' said Zeinab, sensing opposition, 'because that is all they have left. The English have taken everything else from them.'

'What's all this?' said the musician.

'In their music their spirit rises up and defies the hated English.'

'Look, I know that song,' said Owen. 'It's about sheep—'

'They were humble shepherds,' Zeinab told the musician, 'and the British Army came in, just as it came into Egypt, and seized their country and took everything away from them. Except their songs and their spirit.'

'And only in their music can they be free? But that is sad!' said the musician, concerned. 'Sad, but—wonderful! And why is it so sad?' he cried, becoming excited. 'That is how music is! That is how it has always been! The expression of a free people! That is how it was in Italy with the opera. Did you know that, Zeinab? The rise of opera is inextricably linked with the rise of Nationalism. It was so in Italy. It will be so in Egypt. Yes!'

'Yes!' cried Zeinab.

'But where is it now? Where is the Egyptian opera? The true Egyptian opera? It has yet to be written.' Rashid stopped dead. 'I know!' he shouted. '*I* will write it for you, Zeinab! It will have you in it. The spirit of suffering Egyptian woman—'

'Yes!' cried Zeinab enthusiastically.

'And you, my friend!' He turned excitedly to Owen. 'The spirit of nations everywhere, long suppressed and denied! Poor, suffering Wales! I will use some of those soldiers' rhythms. There will be choral singing. Sheep, too. I could put in a pastoral scene—'

Owen gently shepherded them back to the Opera House.

Paul was standing on the steps.

'Hello!' he said. 'What's going on? Zeinab looks a bit excited.'

'She's just joined the Welsh Nationalists.'

'Oh.'

He turned to go in with them but then stopped.

'The Welsh Nationalists? They're not another bunch with a thing about Russia, are they?'

Chapter 5

'Effendi,' declared Selim, 'this is the good life! Little did I think when I entered upon your service what riches it would lead me to! To sit in a café all day drinking coffee while those other poor bastards are out there walking round in the heat—this is bliss indeed!'

'The man is not always upbraiding you?'

'The man *is* always upbraiding me,' conceded Selim, 'but there are compensations.'

Owen did not like the sound of this.

'Keep your hands off the woman!' he said.

'You told me to talk to her!' protested Selim.

'Talk, not touch.'

'Well, Effendi,' said Selim with a grin, 'one thing leads to another.'

'Let it not lead too far! Remember you are here for a purpose!'

'Would I forget, Effendi?' said Selim in wounded tones. 'They have but to stick their heads in here and I will stamp on them!'

'There were other things, too. Like keeping your eyes and ears open. Has anyone come secretly to Mustapha?'

'One came yesterday and wanted to speak with him.'

'What else?'

'Effendi, I do not know. I would have listened but Mustapha sent me out to draw water from the pump. A man like me,' said Selim, injured, 'drawing water from the pump!'

'Never mind that. Did Mustapha speak to you afterwards?'

'He was a right bastard. He kept on at me all morning. And not just me, Mekhmet, too. He dealt Mekhmet a blow, and I thought he would strike me, too, only I rolled up my sleeves and he thought better of it.'

'He said nothing about the man who had come to see him?'

'No, Effendi. But afterwards he had a face like thunder.'

'It is a pity he would not talk with you. You must be friendlier to him.'

'I would rather be friendly with his wife,' said Selim.

'This is important. Find out about the man who came. Find out what was said. If Mustapha will not tell you, talk to his wife.'

'Effendi, I will,' promised Selim. 'I will lure her with words of honey.'

'No doubt. But let them be to the purpose. *My* purpose.'

'You need not fear, Effendi,' said Selim confidently. 'I know how to set about it. In fact, I am already four-fifths there. I have told her how closely you and I have worked together against the gangs. Well, I know that is a little bit of an exaggeration, Effendi, since we haven't worked together against the gangs yet, but the way things are going, it will soon be true. "I know how to handle them," I said to her. "I am sure you do, Selim," she said. "You are so big and strong"—'

'OK, OK.'

'"—and have the ear of the Mamur Zapt," continued Selim, unabashed. '"You have but to say a thing and he pays heed so if you tell him about this Black Scorpion Gang"—'

'What was that?'

'Black Scorpion Gang. You told me to find out, Effendi.'

'Why the hell didn't you—? That's what she said? Black Scorpion?'

'Yes, Effendi. And I said—you'll like this, Effendi—I said, "If we're talking about scorpions, how about a bit of a nip?" And then she slapped my hands—'

'I just wanted to know which was priority, that was all,' said Georgiades.

'The Grand Duke is.'

'I thought the cafés were. They were last week.'

'Protection rackets are always with us. Grand Dukes come and go. Or so we hope.'

'The Grand Duke is obviously priority,' said Nikos, irritated. 'He's got to be, until it's all over.'

Nikos was working on the security arrangements for the Duke's visit. It was the sort of job he liked, abstract, systematic, programmable. His desk was covered with schedules, times down the left-hand side of the page, resources across the top, neatly ruled columns, neat multicoloured ticks. But how did colour fit into Nikos's bloodless systems, wondered Owen? Sparingly, he decided, looking at the columns.

Georgiades continued to grumble.

'I was just getting somewhere on the cafés,' he said. 'That idea of Rosa's was really smart.'

'What idea was this?' asked Nikos, picking up a green crayon and considering it.

'I go round pretending to sell insurance. Against business loss. It works like a charm. They're all interested. It really gets them talking.'

'Do they talk to any purpose?'

'They will,' said Georgiades confidently. 'But I've got to keep at them. That's why I'm asking about priorities.'

Nikos put down the green crayon without using it.

'I can tell you what his priority is,' he said. 'It's sitting in cafés. He's never had a job like this.'

'Don't let the cafés go,' said Owen. 'Only fit your visits in around this business.'

'I was afraid you were going to say that,' said Georgiades.

'Just get on down there!' said Nikos.

Georgiades stood up.

'Find out who organized it and whether there's going to be any follow-up. That's it, isn't it?'

'Yes.'

Georgiades still sought, however, to delay the evil hour; which lasted from about mid morning until the sun began to ease in the second half of the afternoon.

'Tell me,' he said; 'is there any reason why we should treat this more seriously than any of the others?'

'That's what I'm hoping you're going to find out,' said Owen.

⣿⣿⣿

In fact, he had some sympathy with Georgiades, both over the heat—the Babylon was quite some distance away, although Georgiades would use the new electric tram for most of the journey—and over the general question of priorities. It always irritated him when something came up to disrupt the normal pattern of work, something to which others accorded priority. They nearly always had things the wrong way round. In Owen's business, forestalling was a lot better than reacting, and forestalling was largely a matter of careful, continuous intelligence-gathering. Any diversion from that was, in his view, something to be resisted.

This visit of the Grand Duke, for instance, he could have done without. It was an extra. Why go in for extras when you had enough on your plate as it was? He guessed, though, that the Khedive did not see it like that. If you did not like what was on your daily plate you might be more inclined to go in for extras. The occasional circus was what helped you to stomach the bread.

Owen, in unusually puritanical mood, decided that he himself was a bread man rather than a circuses man; and bent his head grimly over a query from Finance.

Some time later Nikos appeared in the doorway. In this heat they always kept the door open. Besides, it improved communication. Owen could monitor what was going on in the office and Nikos could listen in when required to Owen's conversations.

'A Mr. Nicodemus to see you,' he said.

'What about?'

'A tip-off, I think.'

'Oh, right. Show him in.'

Mr. Nicodemus was a short, plump Levantine in the dark suit of the businessman and the normal red, tassled, flower-pot-like tarboosh of the Cairo effendi. He came forward with outstretched hand.

'You won't know me, Captain Owen, but I come to Cairo frequently on business. I am the Levant agent for a large European engineering company.'

He presented Owen with his card, French on one side, Arabic on the other. French was the normal language for business in Egypt, although English was catching on. Mr. Nicodemus spoke in English.

Owen motioned him to a chair and began the usual prolonged courteous enquiries as to health, fatigue and general condition which were the essential preliminary to any Arabic discussion of business. Another indispensable preliminary was the offer of hospitality. A suffragi brought in two little cups of Turkish coffee. Mr. Nicodemus sipped his coffee and praised God and Owen for the flavour; and then business could begin.

'Some time ago,' he said, 'I was contacted and asked if I could supply an urgent order for a client in Egypt. The lack of client details, given the nature of the order, made me'— Mr. Nicodemus paused—'uneasy.'

'What was the nature of the order?'

'It was for explosives.'

'You are in the munitions trade?'

'Yes. Among other things. A small part of our business, actually.'

'And the purchaser?'

'No sale was made. My company does not supply explosives to unknown clients. We said we were unable to supply and I thought no more about the matter. But then this week I learned that one of our competitors had also been approached and had agreed to supply.'

'And that, of course, makes a difference.'

Mr. Nicodemus smiled.

'It does, indeed. My company is all for virtue, Captain Owen, but it hates losing out to those who are less virtuous.'

'Very reasonably. And so you thought you would have a word with me?'

'Exactly!'

'Well, I am interested, Mr. Nicodemus, I must admit. May I ask, though—it is best if we understand each other—are you offering this information...*gratuit*? Or are you looking for...?'

Mr. Nicodemus shook his head hurriedly.

'Oh, no, Captain Owen. Thank you, no. It is being offered purely disinterestedly. I just thought you might like to know.'

'Indeed, I would. As I say, this kind of information interests me considerably. I wonder, though, would you perhaps add a little more detail? About the purchaser, for instance?'

'The person who contacted me claimed to be acting on behalf of an Egyptian quarrying company. But I deal with quite a few quarry companies, Captain Owen, and I know that they do not place orders like that.'

He leaned forward and gave Owen a small slip of paper.

'That was the original specification,' he said.

Owen glanced at it.

'Small,' he said. 'About enough to demolish a small building.'

Mr. Nicodemus nodded.

'I thought, perhaps, a tomb?' he said.

Robbers were always breaking into tombs. Usually they dug their way in. Occasionally, however, they found their way blocked, and then they blasted.

'Perhaps. Can you give me some more details? The delivery date, for instance?'

'One month after signature of contract. But, Captain Owen, that was when they first approached me. They said then that delivery was urgent, so perhaps—'

'Your rival might have agreed to a shorter delivery?'

Mr. Nicodemus nodded.

'It is a small order,' he said. 'It could be supplied from stocks. Then it would be only a question of transport.'

'And entry. It would have to come through customs.'

Mr. Nicodemus spread his hands.

'These things are not always declared,' he said.

Owen glanced at the piece of paper.

'Where was it to be delivered to?' he asked.

'Suez. To await collection.'

'The name?'

'The name on the original specification,' said Mr. Nicodemus, 'was Dhondy. Of course, it may be different now.'

'But Suez, anyway?'

'That, too, might be different. I can, perhaps, help you a little. The name of the supplier is Herbst-Wickel.'

'Your competitor?'

'Exactly.' Mr. Nicodemus gave a little smile.

'Would it be on the shipment certificate?'

'Not necessarily. Not unless they were very foolish.'

'Old labels, perhaps,' said Owen.

'Perhaps. I can tell you one thing more. Herbst-Wickel is asking for payment in gold. It's what you do,' said Mr. Nicodemus deprecatingly, 'when you have doubts about the client. Now, of course, gold can always be obtained, but it takes a little more time and it costs a little more money, and I gather that the client is, or was, having some difficulty.'

Mr. Nicodemus had no more information to impart and shortly afterwards rose to go. Owen thanked him for his helpfulness.

'Not at all,' said Mr. Nicodemus politely.

He hesitated, however, in the doorway.

'It would be nice,' he said, 'if my helpfulness could be remembered. At some convenient moment.'

'Had you a moment in mind?' asked Owen.

'Well,' said Mr. Nicodemus, 'it so happens that we shall shortly be tendering for a contract to supply arms to the Khedivial Army. It is a substantial contract.'

'More substantial than a one-off contract to supply explosives to an unknown client?'

'Certainly.' Mr. Nicodemus smiled. 'You see, I am open with you.'

'It's the best way. Well, I will be equally open with you. I am grateful for your information but I am unable to influence the award of the contract. That is a matter entirely for the Purchasing Department.'

'Of course!' said Mr. Nicodemus hurriedly. 'Of course!' Still smiling, however and still waiting.

At last Owen understood.

'Are Herbst-Wickel also tendering?'

'I believe they are,' said Mr. Nicodemus, now turning definitely to go.

ᘒᘖᘒ

'Were you listening?' asked Owen.

'Yes,' said Nikos.

'What do you think?'

'Genuine.'

'Think we should follow it up?'

Nikos nodded. They usually did with reports of this nature. Explosives was something the administration took seriously. The big users, the quarrying companies and the construction firms working on the dams, were obliged by law to keep explosives under lock and key and notify at once any loss. Others could obtain explosives only in limited quantities and from registered suppliers. All imports were against a licence and licences were normally granted only to registered suppliers. Any report of an illegal import was at once followed up.

But how were they to do it in this case? Owen's resources were already stretched and this business of the Grand Duke was stretching them further. Nikos, who would normally have conducted the enquiry, was busy playing noughts and crosses with the schedules for the Duke's visit. Georgiades, who would usually stand in if Nikos was not available, was already complaining about workloads and talking about priorities. There were others he could use but they were occupied too.

This was precisely the sort of enquiry that suffered when extra things like the Grand Duke came along.

'Shall we leave it for the time being?'

'No, no, no!'

Nikos hated loose ends. If this were not followed up, it would gnaw at him for months.

'It's relatively hot,' he said. 'If we leave it, it will go cold.'

'It's a question of priorities,' said Owen. Heavens, it was catching! 'How important is this?'

'There are some things about it I don't like,' said Nikos.

'Such as?'

'Size. Big enough to blow up a small house. What would it be needed for?'

'Ordinary demolition work?'

'Then why the secrecy?'

'Tomb?'

'All they need for that is a couple of sticks of dynamite.'

'What else, then?'

'A café? A recalcitrant café?' Nikos spread his hands. 'I
don't know,' he said. 'It's just that I'm uneasy. It doesn't fall
into any of the usual patterns.'

This, for Nikos, was the most heinous fault of all.

'Who's buying it, for instance?' he said.

'One of the clubs?'

'They've usually got their own supplies.'

'A new one, then?'

'Well,' said Nikos, 'if that's so, and they're going straight
for explosives, that's very worrying. It's all the more reason
why we should follow it up. Look, I could at least ring round
and see if any of the regular suppliers know anything about it.'

'Well, I'll tackle Customs,' said Owen. 'But that's all!' he
said warningly. 'We have to keep a sense of priorities.'

Jesus, there he was again! It was a disease.

Owen thought about it hard, then took the train to Port
Suez. It would cost him, there and back, two days of valuable
time. Two days! And there he was complaining about his
resources being stretched! But in Egypt if you wanted to get
anywhere you simply had to use a personal approach. Most
of the departments were now equipped with telephones and
Customs, which was one of the most efficient, would certainly
have one. But people were not used to them yet and anyway
it wasn't quite the same. Face to face was what it always came
down to; so train it was, much to Zeinab's disgust, who had
had other things in mind for the following evening.

The train left early, at four, and for the first hour he
watched the spectacular sunrise. The sun came up over the
desert in a great red ball and chased colours for a while across
the sand. But then the colours and the redness disappeared
and everything settled down to a steady monochrome, made
more so by the way in which the tinted windows of the
carriage filtered out the light. The landscape, too, settled

down to monotonous, stony desert, the heat increased, and after that it was a case of grimly hanging on.

It was a relief when at last they got to Suez and he was able to climb down into the fresher, saltier air of the docks. Abdul Shafei, the local Head of Customs, was still in his office. He shrugged.

'We've got a couple of boats coming in,' he said.

He knew Owen by repute and eyed him curiously.

'It's not often that the Mamur Zapt appears in these parts,' he said.

'Cairo's my beat,' said Owen. 'It's not often that I have the chance to get away.'

Water had been brought with the coffee and he drank copiously. Although the air seemed fresher, he found himself sweating profusely. The humidity, he supposed.

He put the glass down and turned to business. Abdul Shafei pulled a pad towards him.

'It should be declared on the certificates,' he said. 'If they do that, there'll be no problem. But what if they don't?'

'Do you open everything?'

'No. There's so much coming in. We open a sample. If it's not in the certification we'll need other identification.'

'Could be difficult.'

'The name of the consignee?'

'It was Dhondy at one time.'

Abdul Shafei made a note.

'But it could have changed. The supplier of the order is a firm named Herbst-Wickel. But, of course, they may be using a shipping agent.'

'You don't know the agent?'

'I could find out the ones they normally use.'

'Please. Anything would help. I'll make a note of the supplier. There may be old labels. Anything else you can tell us?'

'I'm afraid not.'

Abdul Shafei looked doubtful.

'We'll do our best,' he said. 'But—'

'If you could. This is important.'

'Explosives!' Abdul Shafei grimaced.

'Not very nice.'

'Not very nice for us, either,' said Abdul Shafei, 'when we're unloading them and don't know we're handling explosives.'

'The dockers, you mean?'

'Yes.'

Abdul Shafei hesitated.

'Look,' he said, 'I shouldn't be saying this, but…have you thought of talking to the dockers? They know most of what comes into the port. In fact, they probably know it better than we do.'

'I was hoping to keep this fairly quiet. Then I might be able to pick up whoever-it-is when he comes to collect the explosives.'

'Which is more important? Catching the men or catching the explosives?'

'Catching the explosives, I suppose. You reckon it might be worth talking to the dockers?'

'If you really want to be sure,' said Abdul Shafei, 'then talk to the dockers and offer a reward. They open most things that come into the port. There is,' he hesitated, 'well, quite a lot of pilfering. Not more than at other ports, but…I mean, at any port you'll find …'

'Is there some person I should talk to?'

Abdul Shafei looked at him.

'I'm sure there is,' he said. 'But I don't know him.'

Owen walked down to the waterfront, enjoying the smell of sea and tar, the scrunch of pebbles, a different sand. The sea sucked around great wooden posts, gulls cried overhead. As the heat of the day lifted he felt part of a newer, fresher world.

In theory, the Mamur Zapt's writ ran even to Suez. In practice it was confined to Cairo. Cairo was where it all happened. There was a buzz, a life about the city that Owen found it hard to tear himself away from. It was part of an older, more Arab world; cosmopolitan, it was true, but not in the way of Alexandria or the port cities. Suez was hardly a city, still not much more than a bunker port, although growing rapidly. He had no agents here.

He would have to find someone. Nikos normally looked after that side and no doubt would find someone in time. But had they got time?

He sat down on a bollard and watched some dockers unloading a large, seagoing dhow. They were carrying sacks up out of the hold, huge, heavy sacks that bulged. Filled with grain, probably. But why was Egypt importing grain when it had all the fertile land of the Delta?

The men's faces were streaked with sweat. It was hard, hot work. Everything was done by hand. There was an intimacy between the men and the load. That was why they knew the goods so well.

A small boy appeared beside him.

'Effendi, I have a beautiful sister. So ve-ery beautiful!' The boy's hands described improbable shapes. 'Would you like to meet her?'

'No, thanks.'

'Ve-ery good! She make wonderful bump-bump. You like?'

'No, thanks.'

'You prefer boy? I have brother. Handsome! Not like me, Effendi.'

'No, thanks.'

'No boy?'

'No, nor girl, either.'

The urchin was temporarily silenced, while he considered the restricted possibilities.

'Effendi,' he said at last, 'I know a special house. All sorts. You want something different, can do. Dog, perhaps? Donkey? You want donkey?'

Owen turned to give the urchin his full attention.

'What's your name?'

'Sidi, Effendi.'

'Sidi, I am surprised at you. Is this the only way you can make money? I would have thought a resourceful boy like you would be growing fat on the pickings from the docks.'

'Effendi,' said the boy indignantly, 'I am. I get my share. But it is only a small one. Ibrahim says it will be bigger when I can carry a load myself. The men who carry the loads get first choice of the pickings. It wouldn't be fair otherwise. But, Effendi,'—(confidingly)—'I would prefer not to carry the loads. The sacks are heavy and in the sun it is hard work. I would prefer to share in the pickings and not carry the loads.'

'Wouldn't we all. Tell me about your friend, Ibrahim.'

'He carries the loads, Effendi, two, perhaps three, times a week.'

'I would like to meet him. It could be to his advantage.'

'Effendi, I don't know—'

'And yours.'

Owen put his hand in his pocket and jingled some coins.

'Oh, well, Effendi, that's different!'

The boy slipped away and returned some ten minutes later with a thin, wiry man in an embroidered skull cap. Sweat was running down his face and he was mopping his neck with a dirty handkerchief.

'Hard work!' said Owen sympathetically.

'Effendi, I will not deny it.'

'And for not much money.'

'That, too, I will not deny.'

'Even with the pickings.'

'They are few, Effendi. A burst sack, a broken packing case. And then, besides, most of the regular work is with coal and there is not much reward in that.'

'I think I could add to your rewards.'

'What is it you had in mind, Effendi?'

'I need to know if a certain consignment comes in.'

'Will not the office tell you?'

'The consignment I speak of is not likely to be known in the office.'

'It is hidden goods, then?'

'It is likely to have been concealed.'

'That may make it difficult.'

'The reward will be commensurate.'

'I could not do it on my own, Effendi.'

'If the word were spread,' said Owen, 'and what I seek, found, you would take your share. For the finder, the reward would be great. So great that he might not even have to carry loads any more.'

'That indeed would be a reward worth earning.'

Ibrahim stood for some time considering the matter. The sweat was still running down his face. From time to time he dabbed at it with his handkerchief.

'Well, Effendi,' he said at last, 'there is nothing to be lost by doing what you ask and there could be much to gain. I will do it. What is it you ask?'

After he had gone, Owen became aware that the urchin was still standing by him.

'Oh, yes,' he said, and put his hand in his pocket.

Sidi took the coins with surprising inattention.

'Effendi,' he said, 'that reward you mentioned: would it apply to me?'

'If you found what I want, yes.'

'I would buy donkeys,' said Sidi. 'It would be better if they carried the loads, not me.'

'With such an abundance of management insight, Sidi, you are bound to prosper.'

'I hope so, Effendi. Now, about my sister: are you sure—?'

∽∽∽

In the Bab-el-Khalk, the headquarters of the Cairo Police, the heat was stupefying. Owen, working at his desk, had wedged a sheet of blotting paper beneath his writing hand to soak up the persistent trickles of sweat that ran down his arm and threatened to turn everything he wrote into an indecipherable damp smudge. The water in the glass beside him was lukewarm again; only a few minutes before, his orderly had come round to fill the glass with ice. Yusef had said the ice was melting even in the ice house. It had been melting, he said, even when the cart arrived and the men had carried the ice loaves, each tenderly wrapped in sacking, down into the cellar.

The Bab-el-Khalk was as quiet as a morgue. Christ, what would the morgue be doing if the ice was melting! He decided not to think about that. Instead, he changed the image. As quiet as a tomb. Yes, he quite liked that. As quiet as a tomb and as dark as a tomb, with all the shutters closed against the sun, as they had been since early morning.

But not so quiet! Voices, feet running. Someone running along the corridor. The pad of bare feet, the slap of slippers.

Yusef burst into the room.

'Effendi! Effendi! A man—'

A man with his galabeeyah hoisted up round his knees, the better to run, his feet bare, his turban dishevelled, exposing his skull cap, his face running with sweat—'

'Effendi! Mustapha is being attacked again!'

'Mustapha?'

'The café! Oh, Effendi, come quickly! It is terrible!'

Owen jumped to his feet, grabbed his topee—better than a tarboosh if there was a prospect of being hit on the head—and ran out of the room. He found the man running beside him.

'Quick, Effendi! Oh, quick!'

Well, yes, but how? Arabeah? There was a line of the horse-drawn carriages in front of the Bab-el-Khalk but no one would describe them as speedy. Donkey? There would be donkeys tied up in the courtyard, but somehow—Got it! The Aalim-Zapt's bicycle! He ran down into the courtyard. There it was, green, gleaming, modern!

'Tell the Aalim-Zapt!' he shouted, as he sped through the gate.

He hurtled across the Place Bab-el-Khalk. That was easy. It was when he came to the more crowded streets of the native city that he ran into trouble. A massive stone cart was almost entirely blocking the thoroughfare, useless to shout, a little gap at one side—Christ, another one just behind! Another gap, at the expense of a chicken, Jesus, stalls all over the road, onions, tomatoes a few more onions and tomatoes when he'd finished, and now a bloody Passover sheep! Fat, obtuse and in the way! A flock of turkeys, a man carrying a bed, a line of forage camels, three great loads of berseem flopping up and down on either side—steer clear of them—and now a donkey with a rolled-up carpet stretched across its back, the two ends sticking out right across the street, a man sitting on top—! Or was he on top, still? Owen did not dare to look.

He became aware of someone running beside him.

'Nearly there, Effendi!' said the messenger indomitably.

One last street, a crowd outside, well, you'd expect that. He jumped off the bicycle.

'Out of the way! Out of the way!' he shouted.

'Make way! Make way for the Mamur Zapt!' shouted the storyteller.

He pushed his way through. Hands helped as well as hindered.

Suddenly he was through, popped out the front, like a cork out of a bottle.

The café was a scene of destruction. Chairs, tables, hookahs lay all over the floor. In the middle of the room, prone on his face, lay Selim.

Mustapha's wife was on her knees beside him. There was blood all over her *burka*.

'A lion!' she kept saying tearfully. 'A lion!'

Owen bent down. There was a huge gash on the back of Selim's head. Owen bent closer.

'He breathes,' he said.

'A lion!' said the woman, in tears. 'A wounded lion!'

The wounded lion groaned.

'Water!' said the woman. 'Bring water!'

Mekhmet, terrified, plucked at her sleeve.

'Lady,' he said. 'Lady!'

'Fetch water.'

'But, Lady—'

'Go on, you stupid bastard!' said a voice from across the room. It was the owner of the café, Mustapha, pale and limp, sitting exhaustedly on the bottom of the stairs. 'Fetch water, can't you?'

Mekhmet looked around in despair, saw Owen and clutched his arm.

'Effendi! Oh, Effendi!'

'It's all right,' said Owen. 'It's over now.'

'But, Effendi—'

'Get some water, can't you? And after that, some coffee. For me and the Effendi. I bloody need it!'

'Effendi!' pleaded Mekhmet.

'Move your ass!'

Mekhmet fled into the kitchen. Mustapha prised himself up and limped across to Owen.

'A fine bloody job he's done!' he said bitterly, looking down at Selim. 'My café's wrecked! And what did he do about it?'

'He fought like a lion!' said the woman indignantly.

'Maybe, but he fell down like a sheep when they knocked him on the head.'

'And where were you? Under the bed!'

'I've got a broken leg, haven't I? Isn't that enough for you? Or do you want me to get a broken skull as well?'

'It is not for you to chide the one who fought!' said the woman angrily.

'Well, that's his job, isn't it? Fighting? I just wish he'd made a better job of it, that's all.'

'Shame on you!' said the woman. 'While he lies there bleeding!'

'Well, it didn't work, did it? He was supposed to stop this from happening. That was the idea of it, wasn't it? Well, look around you,' he said to Owen. 'A fat lot of use he's been! Protection? Protection, my ass! The only thing he's good for is drinking coffee. You know what? She was more use than he was. Threw boiling water over them!'

'God forgive me!' said the woman.

'God is all-merciful,' replied Mustapha automatically, and then started. 'Here,' he said, 'I hope He doesn't carry it to extremes. We don't want Him forgiving the bastards who wrecked my café!'

Mekhmet appeared from the kitchen with a bowl of water. He put it down and then plucked Owen by the sleeve.

'Effendi,' he said anxiously.

'What about that coffee?' said Mustapha. He picked up a chair and sat down on it heavily. 'There's another for you!' he said to Owen. 'That Mekhmet! Idle as the other one and even more useless! Go and get some coffee, can't you?'

'But, Effendi—' said Mekhmet desperately.

'Coffee!' said Mustapha peremptorily.

Mekhmet looked this way and that and then fled to the kitchen.

Owen turned Selim on to his back. The woman took his head gently on to her knees and began sponging it.

'That's more like it!' murmured Selim.

Suddenly his eyes opened.

'Those bastards!' he said, trying to get up.

The woman pulled him back.

'Well—' said Selim, yielding.

His eyes opened again.

'At least I got one of them!' he said.

Owen glanced around.

'He's not here. They must have taken him away,' he said.

Mekhmet shot gibbering out of the kitchen.

'Effendi—!'

'I threw him in there,' said Selim faintly. 'After I had broken his neck.'

Owen went across to have a look.

'Effendi, he stirs!' said Mekhmet.

'What's that?' said Selim.

'I tried to tell you, but—'

A man was lying among the great jars used for storing water. As Owen looked, a foot twitched.

'Effendi, he lives!'

'Does he?' said Selim, trying to get up. 'I'll soon see about that!'

Chapter 6

The extreme heat continued. In the Bab-el-Khalk next day nothing moved. The orderlies sat stupefied, in the orderly room when they were on duty, outside in the courtyard when they were off. From time to time, Yusef, Owen's own orderly, would pad along the corridor with a fresh pitcher of water, oppressed at the capacity of ice to diminish even in the few yards between the orderly room and Owen's office. Owen, dripping at his desk, was considering whether to change his shirt.

Selim, bandaged, poked his head round the door.

'They're coming now, Effendi.'

Owen could hear the feet at the other end of the corridor, heard, too, a few moments later, Selim's muttered aside.

'Right, you bastard, now you're for it!'

Two slightly apprehensive police constables appeared in the doorway with, between them, rather more apprehensive, the man who had been taken the day before at the café.

Owen looked him over. Nothing very special, just an ordinary fellah in a blue galabeeyah. But that, actually, was significant. It made it less likely that they were dealing with a political club. The Arabs tended to recruit from students and young effendi, or office workers. This man had never seen the inside of a classroom or an office. His hands were big and awkward. Scarred, too. Owen leaned forward and pushed back the man's sleeves. The forearms were scarred also, just where you would expect, and the face, yes, not tribal marks, knife wounds. A tough from the back streets. Owen was almost sure already that this was a criminal gang, not a political one.

The nervousness, too. Members of political clubs might well be nervous when they were brought before the Mamur Zapt but theirs was a different kind of nervousness from that of the ordinary fellah. They were used to the big imposing rooms and the long corridors, which were not so very different from the ones they knew at college or work. If they were nervous it was because of the anticipated consequences, not about the circumstances in which they found themselves.

For the ordinary street criminal it was exactly the reverse. The consequences when they came would be accepted with the immemorial resigned shrug of the fellahin. It was the shock of an environment completely new to their experience that was so disorienting.

Even the toughest of street toughs was put out by the Bab-el-Khalk. There was very little space where they came from. Everything was close, local, intimate. Here in the great open spaces of the Bab-el-Khalk they lost their bearings. Everything was alien to them: the men in their uniforms, the formality, the emotional coldness. Probably most alien of all was the white man they had been brought before.

It was this second kind of nervousness that the man was showing. His eyes flickered compulsively from side to side. It was all new to him. He couldn't make sense of anything.

'What is your name?'

The man looked at him as if he had not understood. As, indeed, probably he had not. Owen doubted if he was taking anything in just at the moment.

Selim leaned over and tapped the man on the shoulder.

'Come on, bright eyes, what's your name?'

What exactly Selim was doing there Owen was not sure. He had appeared shakily that morning and taken up a position in the corridor outside Owen's office, announcing that he wanted to 'see it through'. What 'it' was Owen didn't know. He had an uneasy feeling that Selim was expecting summary execution.

The man, however, seemed to find Selim's intervention reassuring. Perhaps he was used to big constables tapping him on the shoulder.

'Ali,' he said.

'What's the rest of it?'

'There isn't any more.'

'Come on, light of my eyes, don't you have a family?' enquired Selim.

The man seemed bewildered.

'Not as far as I know,' he said.

'You must have!' said Selim. 'You don't suddenly get dropped in the streets.'

'I did,' said the man.

'Don't know your mother?'

'Nor my father, either,' said the man.

Selim turned to Owen.

'Real bastard, isn't he?'

'Just keep quiet, will you?' He was beginning to regret Selim's presence. 'All right, then, Ali, if you don't have a name, do you have a place? Where do you live?'

Again the bewilderment.

'I don't live anywhere,' said the man. Then, as Selim stirred, he added hurriedly: 'I just move around.'

'One woman after another? That it?' said Selim.

'Yes,' said the man. 'That's about it.'

'It's all right for some!' said Selim.

'Shut up! Where did you sleep the night before last?' asked Owen.

'At Leila's.'

'And where will I find Leila?'

'Now we're talking!' said Selim.

Owen wondered whether to throw him out. On the other hand, he did seem to get the man talking.

'I don't know the name of the street,' Ali said.

'Give me the quarter.'

'The Fustat.'

'The Fustat is a big place,' observed Owen.

The man shrugged.

'If I wanted to find you, Ali, where would I ask for you?'

'At Leila's,' said the man promptly, risking a joke and looking to Selim for approval.

Selim, however, did not approve.

'*I'm* the one that makes the jokes,' he said.

The man tried another shrug, which, however, quickly lost confidence.

'Where would I find you?' asked Owen.

'Near the ferry,' said the man reluctantly.

'If I asked for Ali with the scarred face, someone would know?'

'Yes.'

'I expect they'd all know,' observed Owen. 'A man like you!'

Ali responded to the invitation, lifting his shoulders proudly.

'Yes,' he said, 'I'm pretty well known down there.'

'And what about your mates? Are they pretty well known down there, too?'

The man froze.

Owen tried a new tack.

'It's a long way to Babylon,' he said conversationally. Babylon, where the Coptic Ders were, was at the far end of the Fustat. 'What are you doing up here?'

'This is where the money is.'

'Is there not money in the Fustat?'

'Not this kind of money.'

'Still, it's quite a way from the Fustat. Do you often come up here?'

'No,' admitted Ali. 'We usually keep south of the Citadel.'

'But not this time?'

'No.'

'Why not this time?'

'I don't know. I suppose we were offered a job.'

'Ah, you were offered a job?'

Ali closed his lips firmly.

'You wouldn't like to tell me who offered it you, would you?'

'No. I would not.'

'I would be very grateful.'

'My mates mightn't be grateful,' said Ali.

'Ah, yes, but if you helped me you would be out a long time before they were.'

'They would still come out.'

'It would be a long time, though. Of course, you're going to be in for a long time. If you don't help me.'

The man shrugged.

'Well, you think about it. You'll have a bit of time before we get to the trial.'

'I don't even need to think about it,' said Ali.

Owen was virtually certain now that he was dealing with a criminal gang and not a political one. What Ali had said had clinched it. The criminal gangs, as opposed to the political ones, tended to identify with a particular territory and seldom moved off it. And the political clubs, whose aims were more focused, rarely accepted commissions.

He should really now be handing this over to the Parquet. They handled all investigations that were purely criminal. They would have little trouble, he thought, with this one. If Ali was well known down by the docks, the chances were that the other members of the gang would be too. Criminal gangs were local not just in their operations but in their recruitment. Their members would all come from the same neighbourhood, probably from within a few streets of each other. They would make little secret of their membership; in fact, rather the reverse. Membership of a notorious gang was a matter of local pride—again, unlike the political clubs.

'They'll miss you, Ali,' he said, 'down in the Fustat.'

Ali flinched, as if he had received a blow. It was probably the first time that it had come home to him.

'You should think over what I said, Ali. You're going to be away for quite some time. So long that when you come out and go back to the Fustat it will be no good going down to the ferry and asking who knows Ali with the scarred face. Because no one will. As for the Black Scorpion—'

'Black Scorpion?' said Ali. 'What have they got to do with it?'

'That's your lot, isn't it?'

'Is this some kind of trick?' said Ali. 'Look, you can't get me for what someone else has done! That's not fair! That's not justice! Look, I've got my rights!'

'If you're not Black Scorpion,' said Owen, 'then who are you?'

'You know who we are.'

'Just say!'

'The Edge of the Knife. Now are you satisfied?'

❧

'Black Scorpion is what she said,' insisted Selim afterwards, irate. 'Look, Effendi, who do you believe? An idle bastard who goes around hitting people on the head; or a woman so virtuous she goes to the mosque every day and won't let a man put his hands on her?'

'Are you sure that's what she said?'

'Effendi, would I make a mistake on a thing like this? When you had asked me especially?'

'Well, maybe *she* made the mistake, then.'

'Effendi, why waste time? Let me go in and have a talk with that stupid bastard. We'll soon find out who's made a mistake. And it's my guess it's him. As he'll bloody soon discover!'

'Enough! We will go and speak with Mustapha. He's the one who will know. Maybe his wife got it wrong.'

'Effendi—'

Selim fumed all the way to the café.

'Oh, it's you,' said the proprietor unwelcomingly. 'I didn't think we'd be seeing you again. I thought they'd about finished you off.'

'Next time,' promised Selim, with a flash of white teeth, 'they're the ones who are going to be finished off.'

'You'll have to make a better job of it then than you did this time.'

'It was four to one!' protested Selim indignantly.

'It was my mistake,' said Owen. 'I should have left you more men.'

'What, drinking my coffee?' said Mustapha. 'No thanks!'

'Shame on you!' said his wife. 'When the man was ready to lay down his life for you!'

She went across to Selim and gently touched his bandaged head.

'How are you?' she said, concerned. 'It was a grievous wound.'

'Pretty grievous,' Selim acknowledged.

'And you have walked all this way in the heat?'

'Well, yes,' Selim had to admit.

'Oh, Effendi! The man is still weak from his wounds!'

'I do feel a bit weak,' Selim conceded, putting a hand to his head.

'So do I,' said Mustapha. 'Any moment now she'll be giving him my money.'

The woman flashed him an indignant glance.

'Come and sit down,' she said to Selim.

'I could do with a drink,' said Selim.

'Water or coffee?'

'There you are!' cried Mustapha. 'There goes my money!'

'Coffee, please,' said Selim.

She led him off into the kitchen.

'You haven't got any more men outside, have you?' asked Mustapha. 'I mean, I might as well feed the whole Bab-el-Khalk while I'm at it.'

His wife poked her head back into the room.

'God looks after the hospitable,' she said reprovingly.

'Well, I wish He'd make a start, then.'

Mustapha sat down gloomily at a table and motioned to Owen to join him.

'This is very bad for business, you know. People don't like to come here if they think there's a chance of them being knocked on the head.'

'Custom falling off?'

'Not so far,' Mustapha admitted. 'But I'm having to work extra hard to keep it up. I used to get a storyteller in only on slack days. Now I'm paying for one all the time.'

'Eats into profits?'

'Increases the losses. Now there's a thing. Had a chap in this week offering to insure against losses. A fat Greek.'

Owen winced.

'Tempting!' said Mustapha. 'Especially when you're in my position. I said, did it include losses caused by standing out against protection? Certainly, he said. Well, I mean, it's tempting. I mean, we're not getting far as we are, are we?'

'Oh, yes, we are,' said Owen. 'Getting that man yesterday was a breakthrough. Once you've got one member of a gang, it's generally easy to get the others.'

'You think so? You really think so?'

'Oh, yes.'

'Well…well, I hope you're right.'

Mustapha cheered up.

'How about some coffee? Mekhmet! Where are you, you idle bastard? Some coffee for the Effendi! And for me, too, while you're at it!'

He looked around the café with satisfaction.

'Soon get things moving again.'

'I'm sure of that.'

'And you really reckon things might be coming to an end?'

'Yes. He's beginning to talk.'

'Good. Well, take my advice and kick the bastard's balls through the back of his ass. Make sure he talks on!'

'Yes, he's saying things already,' said Owen. 'But one of them has surprised us. I'd just like to check it with you. It's the name of the gang. What was it you told us?'

'I didn't tell you,' said Mustapha.

'But we heard all the same. Black Scorpion?'

Mustapha nodded.

'Are you sure?'

'Look, Effendi, you don't make mistakes on things like that. "Oh dear, sorry, paid the wrong gang. Made a mistake!" It's not like that, Effendi, believe me!'

'I just wanted to be sure.'

'They even wrote it down. The first time. Just so as I would know.'

'Got the note?'

Mustapha heaved himself painfully off his seat and disappeared upstairs. A minute or two later he was back, holding a scruffy piece of paper in his hand.

Owen looked at it.

'This is puzzling,' he said.

'Oh, why? It's the Black Scorpion, isn't it? Look, there!'

He pointed with a grubby forefinger.

'Yes. But the man we've got, the men who came yesterday, were not from the Black Scorpion gang. They were from another one.'

Mustapha sat down heavily.

'*Another* one?'

'So he says. The Edge of the Knife.'

Mustapha was silent for quite some time.

'Two of them,' he said at last. '*Two* of them. God, how many more?'

❦

'"Oh! Oh! Oh!" cried the names as the blind man landed on top of them. The blind man felt the bag with his hands "Got you!" he said triumphantly. There was a long silence, about as long as it takes for a dog to drink a bowl of water, and then one of the names said: "Got who?" "Why, Rice Pudding's new name, of course!" said the blind man. "Ah, yes, but how will you know which one of us it is?" Well, the blind man thought and thought—'

The storyteller was seated on the stone mastaba, or bench, which ran along the front of the café. Around him, some sitting on the mastaba beside him, others on the ground, yet others, detained by the story as they passed by, standing in the street, was a circle of listeners. At the back of the crowd, engrossed, was Selim. Owen edged his way round towards him.

"'I know," he said at last. "I'll feel you." And he put his hand in the bag and caught hold of one of the names. "Get your hands off me, you great, rude, dirty fellow!" said a shrill little voice. "That doesn't sound like Rice Pudding's new name," said the blind man, "and it doesn't feel like Rice Pudding's new name, either. It's all hard and sharp." And he dropped the name back in the bag and caught hold of another one. This one was soft and round. "Hello, big boy!" it said in a low, husky voice—'

'This is beginning to get interesting,' said Selim.

'Now the blind man knew very well that this was not Rice Pudding's new name but he allowed himself to be beguiled. "I'll just have another feel to make sure," he said to himself—'

'Very sensible,' said Selim, ignoring Owen's signals.

'—when, all of a sudden, something wriggled out of the bag and ran off down the street. The blind man made a grab for it but it was too late. Even worse, he had left the top of the bag open and all the other names began to scramble out and run away. All sorts of names came scrambling out of the bag. There were red names and green names, fat names and thin names, old ones and young ones. There were men's names and women's names; and there were names from all the peoples of the world.'

'In the bag?' said someone in the front row.

'Yes.'

'All the peoples in the world?'

'Yes.'

'Including English?'

'Certainly.'

'That doesn't seem right,' objected someone in the second row.

'You've got to draw the line somewhere!' declared a man at the back.

Owen at last succeeded in prising Selim away.

'I've got to go,' said Owen. 'Will you be all right on your own for a bit?'

'Oh, yes, Effendi,' Selim assured him, with a glance over his shoulder towards the kitchen.

'I'll send some more men down. I can only spare two for the moment, unfortunately. We're very stretched just now.'

'Send Abdul, Effendi. He's simple but strong. And Fazal. He's a mean bastard, just the man.'

'I'll do my best. I don't think they'd better be actively in the café, though. It would be too noticeable. Perhaps they'd better hang around outside. Not in uniform, obviously.'

Selim didn't like this.

'Effendi, it's bad for those idle bastards to have nothing to do. Especially when I'm working. Look, I've got a better idea. My wife's got a cousin, he's a Nubian wrestler, big, really big, half savage, too, they're all like that down there. It's all right in the women, adds a bit of something, you know— where was I? Oh, yes, Babakr. Well, as I say, he'd break your back as soon as look at you. Now, for a few piastres—'

ॐ

'So,' said Mahmoud, 'you think it's a criminal gang, do you?'

Owen nodded.

'Pretty sure. It's based on the Fustat. The man we took yesterday comes from near the ferry and I wouldn't be surprised if the rest did too. They don't operate outside the Fustat much, which is another thing that makes me think they're not a club. The clubs stick mostly to the schools and El Azhar all in the modern city, and that's where the targets are, too. This chap said they kept south of the Citadel.'

'What were they doing up here, then?'

'Someone asked them to do a job for him. Actually, I'd like to know about that. Who asked them and why? It could still be political.'

Mahmoud nodded. In principle—and Mahmoud was the sort of man for whom principles stick up all over the place—the distinction Owen was making was one that he could not accept. The Parquet, in his view, should be responsible for all judicial investigation and he objected strongly to the Mamur Zapt having reserved powers in cases where a political dimension was suspected. In practice, he understood the distinction very well.

'So,' he said, 'what is it that you are proposing?'

'Well, in the ordinary way of things, if I thought something was criminal, I'd pass it over to the Parquet. But there's a question mark about this.'

'Who commissioned the job?'

'Yes. But not just that.'

He told Mahmoud about the possibility that a second gang was involved.

'I suppose I ought to hang on to it until I'm sure, but the fact is I've got a lot on at the moment and if it's just criminal I'd rather hand it over to the Parquet right away. There's work to be done on it and if we hang around it might all go cold.'

'Pass it on, by all means,' said Mahmoud amiably.

'The trouble is, I'm not absolutely sure. The other gang, you see, if there *is* another gang, might turn out to be a political club. I was wondering—is there any possibility of your taking this on yourself? Then if there turned out to be a political dimension we could probably handle it between us, and if there wasn't, well, so much the better.'

Mahmoud considered. In principle he was against this kind of thing. It blurred lines of responsibility; by agreeing you suggested that you condoned the system; and it was all horribly pragmatic. Mahmoud, again on principle, was against pragmatism. There was too much of it about and it mucked up system. And system was what Egypt all too plainly needed. On the other hand, the system was clearly mucked up and you had to do what you could.

'Well,' he said, weakening, 'I suppose you could say I'm already involved.'

'Already?'

'So far as cafés are concerned. Those soldiers the other night,' he supplemented.

'You're still on that?'

'I certainly am. There is a major issue of principle—yes, well, I'm still pursuing it. But as to getting your case assigned to me if you transferred it—well, I could probably arrange it—'

They got down to details. Ali, it was agreed, would be handed over to Mahmoud as soon as the case was formally transferred. Selim would be left for the moment where he was. As for reinforcements, Mahmoud, to Owen's surprise, favoured the Nubian wrestler.

'It's only a few piastres,' he said. 'Wouldn't your budget stand it?'

'Well, yes, but—'

Experience had, however, given Mahmoud a realistic sense of the rival merits in a brawl of the average Cairo constable and a Nubian wrestler.

'The Nubian wrestler every time,' he said, 'especially if Selim has a few more friends like him. Besides, it's better if they're not too obviously policemen.'

Owen promised to have a word with Selim.

At the end they sat back.

'Of course,' said Mahmoud, 'this doesn't alter the principle.'

'Principle?'

'That there should be just one body responsible for investigation.'

'That's what the Army thinks too,' said Owen.

⌒ᙡᙡᕲ

Back in his office, Owen felt pleased. He would have liked to have kept the café business to himself just a little longer, but Mahmoud would handle it all right and meanwhile he really ought to be concentrating on the Grand Duke's visit. Nikos was finalizing arrangements but they would need to be talked through with the people concerned and he himself would have to do that. The procession remained the real problem, the time when Duke Nicholas would be most at risk, but Owen had cunningly delegated entire responsibility for that to the Army. 'Unified command,' he had muttered, and Shearer, dumb idiot that he was, had nodded agreement. So if anything went wrong he was the one who would get it in the neck.

In fact, judging by the reports of Owen's agents, the various protest meetings were unlikely to issue in anything serious. The groups which had come together had promptly fallen apart. Only down in the Babylon, according to Georgiades, were there still rumours of action. The committee formed there after the public meeting which Owen had witnessed was still divided over its terms of reference. However, some of the more vehement members, including Sorgos, had walked out and it was rumoured that they had set up a caucus which was pressing ahead with ideas for action. Owen decided to go and see Sorgos.

It was not Sorgos, however, who opened the door but Katarina.

'The Mamur Zapt?' she said, surprised.

'Again!' said Owen.

'My grandfather is not in.'

'That may not be a bad thing.'

'Oh?'

She looked at him suspiciously.

'What sort of visit is this?' she demanded.

'It's not matrimonial, anyway.'

Katarina started to smile, then caught her lip.

'He has been to the bazaars. I am expecting him back at any moment,' she said. 'You may come in.'

All over the floor were papers.

'What are these?' asked Owen.

'Stories.'

'Stories?'

'I handle that side of the business while my father is away. Are you interested in stories?'

'There is one I especially like. It is one of the Sultan Baybars stories. Its chief character is a man named John. He's a Europeanized Christian who happens to have studied Muslim law. On the strength of this he wangles his way into being Kadi of Cairo and then from this position as supreme Law Giver he proceeds to subvert all the laws. A sort of Mamur Zapt figure.'

Katarina giggled.

'I recognize the story,' she said. 'Just.'

'Allow for a little subversion,' said Owen.

Things were getting promising but just then there were sounds at the door.

'My young friend from the mountains!' cried Sorgos delightedly.

Katarina scuttled out, all confusion. Sorgos looked at her retreating back in surprise; then with sudden miscomprehension.

'Ah!' he said, pleased. 'I have returned too soon!'

'Not at all! Not at all!' said Owen hastily.

Sorgos came into the room. As he stepped forward without his stick he stumbled slightly, overbalanced by the large bag he was carrying.

Owen sprang forward.

'Let me assist you!' he said, putting his hand under the old man's arm and taking the bag from him.

'It is nothing,' said Sorgos, letting Owen's arm take his weight, however.

Owen helped him to the divan and eased him gently down on it.

Sorgos looked at the bag a trifle anxiously and Owen put it down beside him. It was extraordinarily heavy. But that was not surprising. For Owen had looked inside the bag and seen what it contained. Gold dust.

Chapter 7

Owen took an arabeah at the Place Ataba-el-Khadra and drove down the Musky, the long street which connects the European with the other quarters, until he reached the area of the bazaars. Just before the Turkish bazaar he turned left into the Khordagiya but there the way became so blocked with people, carts, stalls, donkeys and camels that he dismounted and paid off the driver. He was in any case almost at his destination: the goldsmiths' bazaar.

The street at that point was lined with the showcases of the goldsmiths hard at work at their smithing in the narrow, dark lanes of the bazaar. For much of the manufacture was actually carried on in the bazaar itself. It was not just a place for selling. The smiths had their workshops in the little, three-feet-wide lanes that ran back off the Khordagiya and in the darkness you could see the flames from their braziers and the little lights of their blowpipes.

The area was so densely packed with people that it was difficult to move. All of them were Egyptian—the tourists made straight for the Turkish bazaar opposite—and most of them were women, heavily veiled and in featureless black; only, incongruously, their ankles showed beneath their heavy robes. And that, in fact, was the point, for almost every single one of the women wore heavy silver or gold anklets which she was anxious to display. Owen, once, taken by the workmanship, had bought one of them for Zeinab, thinking it a bracelet. Zeinab had patted him on the head and told him to give her the money next time. Between the chic Zeinab and her sisters there was something of a gap, which, she pointed out, despite his efforts, she was anxious to preserve.

The more ordinary women of Cairo liked to carry their wealth, such as it was, about with them. No keeping it safe in dark corners for them! Perhaps surprisingly, their husbands concurred, feeling, possibly, that in this way at least their wealth was under their eye. Whatever it be, the fact was that almost every woman, except for the very poorest, carried around with her a considerable weight of gold and silver on her feet. And the goldsmiths' business thrived!

There they were now, the women, almost indistinguishable as individuals in the shadows in their black, massed in front of the open, glassless cases, inspecting the anklets, bracelets, necklets, talismans, rings and even diadems (when did they get a chance to wear these, Owen wondered?), all in filigree and almost all in unusually pure metal. The women's tastes ran to the heavy, the solid and the barbaric and the work did not correspond at all to the inclinations of the tourists, who preferred the Europeanized shops of the large bazaars where the work was more delicate if far pricier.

Owen began to move down the lanes, taking his time, stopping to chat in each workshop. In his tarboosh, and with his dark Welsh colouring, he might well have been an Egyptian; not a policeman, certainly.

Eventually, he found the one he wanted. Yes, an old man, not Egyptian, not Greek, something in between, Turkish, perhaps, had called asking about gold.

'Funny thing to ask for, isn't it? That's why I remember. You'd expect him to go to one of the suppliers. But he didn't seem to know about them. I didn't tell him, either—you don't give all your trade secrets away, do you? Not if you've any sense. Maybe he's thinking of starting a business up of his own; not him, perhaps, but a son, say, or a son-in-law. We've got enough people in the trade as it is, we don't want any more.'

A funny thing to ask for, Owen agreed. Had he said what he wanted it for?

'They're working on some ikon. Down in one of the churches. Or so he said. "In that case," I said, "you'll not be wanting brick, you'll be wanting dust." No, he said, he'd prefer brick. "Well," I said, "you're probably not an expert, but I'm pretty sure that what you really need, if it's an ikon you're talking about, is dust. In any case, dust is all I can let you have. I get plenty of that left over. But if you're talking about material to work, well, I only get as much as I need. You've got to pay cash." Well, he went away, but then he came back and said he'd like dust. I sold him some but then he wanted more and I said, I haven't got any more, not for a week or two, that is. And he said, it'll be too late then. So I said, you'd better go and ask someone else, then. And that's what he did, I think.'

'Can you sell dust?'

'Oh yes. There's some people who want it. But what would be the point of selling it, if he's only just bought it? And bought it from the likes of me? I mean, we're not going to let him have it cheap, are we? I wouldn't say we're making a fortune out of it, but it's not in our usual line of business and you naturally charge a bit extra. He ought to go direct to a supplier. But then, if he did that, they'd always be able to undercut him, wouldn't they? If he was trying to sell it on!'

Owen agreed it was a funny business and asked how much dust the old man had purchased.

'How many ikons is he doing?' he said. 'This seems a lot, if there's only one.'

'And he wanted more! "You'd better check your particulars," I said. "With gold, you want to get it right."'

'You certainly do,' agreed Owen. 'Did he say which church it was?'

'No. It's down in the Babylon somewhere.'
'Oh!' said Owen. 'The Babylon?'

⚬∽∽⚬

Owen had arranged to meet Georgiades in the old Greek cathedral. Arriving a little early, he climbed up to the roof to orientate himself. Babylon was spread out below him. Right at his feet were the vineyards which sheltered the seven ancient churches; and, at this height, the walls of the Ders, the fortified precincts, were plainly visible. At ground level it was sometimes difficult to distinguish them. Within the walls the people were going about their daily business: the little boys to school, the women to the pumps and wells for water, or perhaps making an early visit to the *suk*, the men to the little shops and workshops often set in recesses of the walls to begin their day's work. Beyond the houses in one direction he could see the Nile, and Roda Island, with its Nilometer, and the ferry crossing the river, and on the other side the village of Gizeh and the pyramids. Turning round, he could see Saladin's great aqueduct stealing along the sandhills of the Fustat until it reached modern Cairo with its minarets and domes and Saladin's Citadel on its rock.

It was against the Muslim invaders that the Copts had built the Ders. For the Copts had been here before the Arabs, before even the Romans. They were the original inhabitants of the place and had clung on to their identity despite successive waves of invaders. Was there not a lesson here for Sorgos, Owen wondered?

If there was, he was not sure that he liked it. For the Copts had survived by going underground: underground literally, beneath and behind their great walls, but underground in other ways too, burying themselves in the general population, distinguishable by their clothes and their features, but never seemingly asserting themselves. If there was a nationalism here, it was a secret, covert one, though perhaps none the less tenacious for that.

Owen preferred to look at the Ders from up here. At
ground level he had too much of the feeling of being in a
ghetto. You were too conscious of the walls barring out the
rest of the world. And everything seemed somehow underground. It was an effect, perhaps, of the architectural search
for shade, but it made everything dark, claustrophobic.

He heard footsteps on the stairs. Georgiades emerged,
breathing heavily.

'Grandmother's pleased,' he said.

'What?'

'Pleased at me coming here,' he said. 'To the cathedral.
She thinks there's hope yet.'

'I didn't know you had a grandmother.'

'Not mine, Rosa's. She used to come here regularly when
the family first came to Egypt. They lived down here for a
while before moving up to the city.'

He came across to the parapet and stood beside Owen.
The catheral was built into a bastion of the old Roman
fortress.

'It's the vineyards, too. Like home, she says. Greece.'

He bent over the parapet.

'It's over there,' he said, pointing.

'Al-Mo'allaka? The church where they're restoring ikons?'

'Yes. You can't really see it from here.'

'I've been there, I think.'

'If you had, you'd remember it. Shall we take a look?'

They went back down the stairs and out into the cloisters.
Within a few yards Owen lost his bearings. Cloisters became
tunnels, tunnels, dark alleyways and then cloisters again. They
went through underground arcades where the shops were
illuminated only by candles. Eventually they emerged into
sunlight, the sunlight of a small palm-tree court with a
fountain in its middle. From one end of the court a staircase
led upwards. Al-Mo'allaka, the Hanging Church, was at the
top of that.

The church got its name not from the fact of being actually suspended, but from its having been built high up in one of the ancient gateways of the old Roman fort. To reach it you had to climb up the staircase. At the top was a kind of atrium and the church opened off this.

Owen stopped for a moment in the doorway to let his eyes get used to the darkness. The church was lit by old hanging lamps and the light that came from their tiny flames was hardly enough at first for him to be able to make anything out. But then he saw the antique columns of marble taken, so Georgiades said, from some Roman temple, which broke the space up into the traditional three parts of a Coptic church: the place of the women, the place of the men, and the place of the priests. Gradually he became aware of the old barrel roof, bolted to open woodwork like the timbers of a ship: and then of the low Moresco arches, outlined in ivory, which led to the sanctuary. His eye came back to more marble, that of an incredibly finely carved pulpit, very long and narrow, standing on delicate marble shafts. Only very slowly, because of the darkness of the wood, did he become aware of the backdrop to everything, a screen which, unusually, ran right round the church and which seemed, unbelievably, to glow in the darkness.

He went forward into the church and saw that the screen was covered with golden ikons. The gold caught the light from the swinging lamps and seemed both to absorb and reflect it, to take it into itself as a kind of inner energy and then to release it again, slowly.

Georgiades touched his arm. At first he did not see, but then Georgiades pointed and he realized that over in a corner a man was working on one of the ikons.

They went across. The man looked up. Owen couldn't see him well but saw enough to know that he was not an Arab. Or a Copt, for that matter.

'Fine work!' said Owen.

'Just the finishing touches,' said the man. They spoke in Arabic but although the man spoke it well, it was not his first tongue. 'We do most of the work in our workshop out the back.'

'You have a lot of work here, then?'

The man nodded.

'We are working on five. Just restoring, of course.'

'Difficult, with the materials. Is that real gold?'

The man smiled.

'Dust,' he said, 'fixed with paint. I wouldn't try to get it off.'

'Still,' said Owen, 'not cheap!'

'We're the ones who are cheap,' said the man, cheerfully, however.

'Even you have to be paid for, though.'

'There is a cost,' the man agreed.

'I didn't know the Church was that rich,' said Owen.

'Oh, this kind of thing isn't paid for by the Church. It's financed by donations.'

'And someone has given the money for you to do these?'

'Enough for five of them only, unfortunately.'

'Well, I suppose the cost adds up. I mean, the dust by itself…How much dust would you need to do a job like this?'

'Very little,' said the man. 'That's why it's not worth your trying to take it off!'

Owen laughed.

'I'll have to find some other way of getting rich.'

They stood watching the man for a little while.

'The workshop's out the back, if you'd like to put your head in.'

Owen followed Georgiades down the stairs and out into the court with the palm trees and the fountain. A high wooden trellis of fine old *meshrebiya* work divided off a small garden at one end, on the other side of which were what looked like low cloisters. A man was working in one of them.

'Just been talking to your mate upstairs,' said Owen.

'Oh, yes?'

The man stayed bent over his work. It was another ikon and he was gently brushing the face. Out here in the daylight the ikon seemed flatter, had lost its glow.

'Difficult work,' said Owen.

'Not when you know how.'

'Ah, yes, but it's the knowing how! Not many people with your skills, I fancy.'

'Not many,' said the man, 'but too many.'

'Too many for the jobs available?'

'You could say that.'

'Churches aren't the best customers. Still, from what your mate was saying, someone else is paying this time.'

'Lucky for once.'

'A sick patron?'

'A dead patron. This was a bequest.'

'Ah, so there won't be any more when it's finished?'

'That's right.'

They watched for a while and then turned away. Back up in the church a priest was lighting candles.

'The bequest? All very fine, but it won't buy salvation. Not by itself, that is. God isn't bribable. Though Arturos probably thought he was. He certainly thought everyone else was.'

'It's a genuine bequest, then?'

'In what sense?'

'The church has actually received the money?'

'Oh, yes.'

'And decided to allocate it to restoration of the ikons? Or was that Arturos's idea?'

'Ours.'

'Ah! A considerable sum?'

'Considerable in Arturos's eyes.'

'Enough to restore five ikons?'

'That's about it.'

'The materials are costly,' Owen observed.

'We're used to tight budgeting.'

'And Arturos himself, what sort of man was he? Interested in the Church?'

'When he thought he was going to die, yes.'

Owen laughed.

'A lot of us are like that.'

'Everyone is like that,' said the priest.

He walked with them to the door. In the court everything was still. Even while they had been inside, it had grown appreciably hotter.

They heard the tap of boots on the atrium, unusual in a world of slippers and bare feet. A man appeared at the top of the staircase.

'One of the workmen?'

'A friend of theirs, I think.'

First, the boots, and then the face; Owen recognized the man who had run after Sorgos on the night of the boisterous public meeting in the Der.

∽∾∾∾

'It *must* be,' said Nikos. 'Nicodemus said that Herbst-Wickel was insisting on payment in gold. It must be for the explosives.'

'One thing's for sure,' said Georgiades; 'it's not for the ikons. The amount they need is nothing like the amount he's getting.'

'It's got to be the explosives. What else would he want gold dust for?'

'It's a hell of a clumsy way to get gold, though, isn't it?' said Owen.

'Ah, yes,' said Georgiades, 'But—don't you see?—he's never done it before. It's not something you buy everyday. Take me, for instance: I never buy gold. You buy gold?' he asked Nikos.

Nikos sniffed disdainfully.

'If I did,' he said, 'I'd know how to go about it better than he does.'

'Very amateurish,' said Owen.

'Ah, yes, but, you see, he *is* an amateur. It's the first time he's ever done anything like this. The same with all of them, probably. Never bought gold, never bought explosives, never even tried to kill a Grand Duke before!'

'Why did they pick on explosives, then? Why not just try and shoot him?'

Nikos shrugged.

'Perhaps they wanted to make sure.'

'The danger is,' said Owen, 'that they try to make too sure and send a lot of other people with him. Explosives are not for amateurs. God knows who they might blow up!'

'The way they're going,' said Nikos, 'they're not going to be in a position to blow anyone up, not by the time the Grand Duke gets here, anyway. Not if it depends on Sorgos acquiring enough gold to pay for the explosives. If you look at what he must have been able to get in this ham-fisted way, he must still be miles short.'

'That's our big hope.'

'Well,' said Georgiades, 'if it all depends on Sorgos, isn't the solution obvious?'

'Take him in, you mean?'

'Someone else might do it then,' said Nikos, 'someone who's more efficient.'

'In any case,' said Owen, 'I'm hoping he's going to lead us to the rest of the people involved. You've got someone on him?'

'Yes,' said Nikos. 'Apparently he's still buying.'

'That's good. Don't forget, Herbst-Wickel want payment in advance. It means they've still not got the explosives.'

☙

Owen had hoped that, having passed the case over to Mahmoud, for the time being he could forget about protection gangs, but early the next morning he received an agitated summons from Mustapha.

'What's the trouble?'

'Two!' said Mustapha, shaking his head disbelievingly. 'Two on the same night!'

'Two what?'

'More demands from the gangs. I thought you said everything was going to be all right?'

'It will be. Don't worry. Who were they from?'

'The same as before. One was from the Black Scorpion. You know, like the first time. The other was one of those who came the other time, you know, the time they beat that dope up.'

He inclined his head in Selim's direction. Selim, however, was unmoved. Indeed, he was positively beaming.

'This is getting beyond a joke!' said Mustapha. 'I don't mind paying protection to one gang, or, rather, I do, but there's not much I can do about it. But I can't pay protection to everyone in Cairo!'

'Don't worry. I'll look after it.'

'Well, I should hope you would. I pay my taxes, you know. Or, at least, some of them. That's another bunch of robbers for you! It's about time I got something back.'

'Don't worry. You won't have to pay. I'll see to it. Or, at least,'—remembering that Mahmoud was now supposed to be looking after this end of things—'I'll talk to someone who will.'

'Oh, yes,' said Mustapha sceptically. 'Passing the buck, are you?'

'No. I'll get on to him right away. Meanwhile, you've got Selim. And friends.'

'Friends?' said Mustapha, scandalized. 'You mean that?'

He drew Owen to the door and pointed along the street. A hulk lying in the shade raised an arm in acknowledgement.

'He looks big enough,' said Owen.

'Oh, he's big enough, all right. If he could only manage to drag himself to his feet. And the only time he does that is when he comes in here and asks for something "to keep him going". Well, I'd like to keep him going, all right, going some-where else, fast. Protection racket? This man's a protection racket all on his own!'

'Only coffee, I hope?'

'*Only* coffee? Look, coffee costs money, as well as all the other things my wife gives him. Another of these down-and-outs she can't resist! I tell you, I'm feeding half the population. And the other bloody half is sending me protection notes!'

At last Owen managed to get away. He had just turned the corner when he heard himself hailed by Selim.

'Effendi! Effendi!'

'Yes?'

'Effendi, there is much to report!'

'Report away, then.'

'Effendi, I saw those men last night. Including that little bastard who was one of those who attacked me the other day. And I said to myself: I will stave that man's head in! But then, Effendi, I reflected. Am I not a policeman, I said to myself? Do not I serve the Mamur Zapt? And would he wish me to do a thing like that? Surely not. He would wish me to hold back until I could stave in the heads of *all* the bastards. So, Effendi,' said Selim, swelling with pride, 'I held back!'

'Good for you. Now—'

'Then, Effendi, I thought more. These are evil men, I said, and they will come again. And when they come again, by God, this time I will be ready and I will level the score. And the good thing is, I don't have to go to them; they will come to me. All I have to do is sit here on my backside. That was pretty good thinking, wasn't it, Effendi?' said Selim anxiously.

'Pretty good. Now—'

'I put it to Babakr. That was Babakr up the street, Effendi. I think you saw him?'

'Yes, indeed.'

'Well, I put it to him and he thought it was a good idea too. He said, it's better that the mountain should not go to

Mohammed, especially if it's very hot, but that Mohammed should come to the mountain. And then we can throw the bloody mountain at him. That was a good thought, wasn't it, Effendi? I must say, I'd never thought of Babakr as a religious man before, but that was pretty good.'

'Yes, well, thanks, Selim—'

'But that is not all, Effendi. When the second man came, that little bastard who was here the other day, I said to myself: I will not stave his head in, but is it right that I should let him go? If I miss the chance, I may lose him forever. I may never see him again. But if one were to follow him home, so that I would know where to look for him—'

'You followed him home?'

'Well, no, Effendi, not I. I'm the one who has the ideas. It is for other people to do the walking. So I told Mekhmet—'

'Mekhmet followed him?'

'Yes, Effendi. He was at first unwilling—Effendi, the man is but a hollow reed—but I persuaded him. So if you would like to give him a piastre, no more, the man's not worth it, but I wouldn't mind a couple for myself, Effendi—'

'Just a minute,' said Owen. 'Are you saying that Mekhmet followed this man all the way home?'

'That's right, Effendi. It was a bad place they went to, down in the Babylon—'

'Fetch Mekhmet,' said Owen.

Chapter 8

Babylon, or Bab-el-On, the Old City, had been there before
the Muslims came. Its original inhabitants had been the
Copts, lineal descendants of the Egyptians in the time of the
Pharoahs. Over the centuries they had become Christians
and the Ders were essentially Christian enclaves against the
Muslim invaders. The Muslim tide had swept over the original
fortified churches destroying the forts but leaving the
churches, and it was in their precincts that Christians had
traditionally gathered. Over the years many Copts had moved
out, up to the modern, more prosperous city of the Arabs,
but in their place had come other Christians: Greek (which
was why there were almost as many Greek churches as there
were Coptic in Babylon), Macedonians, Montenegrins and
Serbians. Most recently there had come Georgians. Here, too,
a generation ago, had come the Mingrelians; and with them
had come Sorgos.

It was in one of the Ders that, with the instinct for alliance
characteristic of the new immigrant, he had settled when he
had made the journey from his native Caucasus. There he
had found his first job, incongruously, perhaps, as an appren-
tice bookbinder, although one should remember that he was
familiar with leather-working. There, in time, he had opened
his own workshop. In the same Der he had bought his house
and it was there that his son had been born. The Der was

where his roots lay; and the place in which, when the time came, he naturally looked to for allies.

Georgiades had been ferreting them out. The people who had known Sorgos in the early years were now mostly dead but acquaintance had been preserved in their families, was a kind of family matter, and Sorgos was still well known in the Der.

Yes, he came here often. Not, perhaps, as much as he did, for it was a long way to travel. When his son had opened the bookshop near the Clot Bey, he had moved with him.

It was in the bookshop that Katarina had been born. The world she had grown up in was very different from that of the Der. Her father, quickly literate, had slipped easily into the Europeanized culture which his trade had opened up to him. Mingrelian, he was still, but Cairo, now, and even Paris, was his intellectual home and not the Caucasus.

The mother? Mingrelian, of course, and apparently very beautiful. She had died giving birth to Katarina. Her daughter, after the earliest years, had grown up in a household without women, one in which she was actually closer to her father and his world than to her grandfather and the closed world of the Der.

The Der, said Georgiades, was the thing, not the Mingrelians. They were scattered now around Cairo and there were not many of them. Sorgos, as senior elder, commanded great prestige and the few Mingrelians left worked dutifully to preserve their language, but community they hardly were. Most of them had been assimilated into other communities which were now for them more important. Sorgos might still eat patriotic fire but the attention of the other Mingrelians had passed to other pursuits. A few had been disposed to join him in his Crusade against the Grand Duke but, said Georgiades, the fact that the original public meeting had been held in the Der was not coincidental. It was there, not amongst the Mingrelians, that Sorgos expected to find his allies.

'Not among the Copts,' said Nikos. The Copts, who had survived through the centuries by keeping their heads down, were not going to stick them up for the sake of parvenus.

'And not among the Greeks, either,' said Georgiades.

It was on the others that Georgiades had concentrated his enquiries and he had very soon found out the men Sorgos had recently been seeing.

'He went round the lot, Serbs, Albanians, Caucasians, and most of them were prepared to join him on the platform for that first meeting. It was after the meeting that the problems began. They couldn't work together. In the end he walked out in disgust.'

It was the Georgians, mostly, who had walked with him. Their wrongs were fresher in their minds, the wounds inflicted by the Russians still raw. The men were younger; and in Djugashvili, the man who had run after Sorgos when that first public meeting had ended, Georgiades thought that they might have found a leader.

'Just a minute,' said Nikos, frowning, 'have you got anything definite?'

'No,' said Georgiades. 'It was just that when I asked, everyone said that he was the man the Georgians naturally turned to.'

'He wasn't on the platform,' said Owen.

'No. They don't really amount to a sizeable community. There are even fewer of them than there are of the Mingrelians. And there doesn't seem to be any community leader. The fact is,' said Georgiades, 'I don't think they *want* to become a community. They want to go back to Georgia.'

'So the war against Russia is still real to them?'

'That's right. So far as they are concerned, it's never ended. Retreat to Egypt is just a temporary tactical withdrawal.'

'And the Grand Duke fair game?'

'Undoubtedly.'

'There's still nothing definite,' said Nikos.

Georgiades turned to him.

'The gold?' he said. 'Isn't that definite?'

'All we know,' said Nikos, 'is that Sorgos is buying gold dust. Which might or might not be used to buy explosives. What's the connection with the Georgians?'

'They provide the excuse. Sorgos would never have thought of it. It had to be someone who knew about working on ikons. And these people do.'

'It's not enough,' said Owen. 'Yet.'

∽

'Why are you pursuing me?' demanded Katarina.

'I'm not pursuing you,' said Owen.

'It's just an accident that you're here, is it?'

'That's right. There are a lot of them about.'

Katarina moved on to the next stall and began to finger the water melons.

'Is he bothering you, lady?' asked the stallkeeper.

'I'm her brother,' Owen assured him.

Katarina tossed her head indignantly. She was dressed in shapeless black but the shapelessness failed to deny entirely the shape that was beneath and it was this, perhaps, though he hoped not, that had originally caught his attention. Her hair, that most provocative of features for the Muslim, was completely covered and she wore a long veil over the lower part of her face. However independently she might dress at home, going to the *suk* she took care to dress in exactly the same way as her sisters. Invisibility, at least in public, was what was required of women.

Naturally enough, in the circumstances, they all observed it. The *suk* was full of at first sight indistinguishable black-clad forms. Naturally, too, though, most of them subtly denied it. If their hair was covered, their ankles were bare and, as in the goldsmiths' bazaar, around every shapely ankle was a ton of hardware. Not, of course, in the case of Katarina, and was the face quite as fully covered as in the case of the other women? It was her eyes which, close to, had finally given her away.

Somewhat to Owen's surprise, another man approached her as she stood at the stall. He appeared to know her, for he greeted her warmly.

'You haven't been to see us for a long time, Abbas,' she chided him.

'Well, no. I've not been working anywhere near the shop, and with your father away—'

Owen had worked out now that he was a storyteller. He wore the *mukleh*, the unusually wide, rather formal turban which in old times had marked out the men of letters, a status which storytellers, sometimes unjustifiably, always claimed, but other items of his dress, the rather worn *farageeyah*, or top robe, suggested a man of letters fallen on hard times.

'Are things going well?'

'People are interested, all right. They like the stories. They're a bit of a change. Only the old lot with their romances are so well established that it's hard to get a foot in. There's a lot of resistance, I can tell you.'

'You'll just have to keep at it.'

'Yes, I know. Your father was right. It's the only way.'

'Are you all right for stories?'

The man fumbled beneath his robes and produced a handful of rather tattered papers.

'Excellent!' said Katarina. 'Well, when you need some more—'

The storyteller bowed politely and moved away.

'Shameless!' said the stallkeeper indignantly. 'Allowing herself to be spoken to by men!'

'I know!' said Owen. 'That's the problem, really. That's why I, as her brother—'

Katarina gave him a furious glance and stalked off, head held high.

Owen followed her, at a distance, as she went round the stalls completing her shopping. When she had finished, he stepped up to her.

'Carry your bags, miss?'

Kataiina looked at him levelly.

'That *would* create a disturbance!' she said. 'To have a man doing the carrying!'

She marched through the stalls to the edge of the *suk* and then set off down a side street. Owen drew alongside her.

'If you are going to insist—' she said.

'Just a word.'

'You'd better walk in front, then.'

He drew two paces in front of her and she took up the woman's customary position.

'I'd forgotten you were in the storytelling business.'

'Story-selling!' she corrected. 'Not telling.'

'They come to you for stories?'

'Yes.'

'Well, I am disillusioned. I thought they all came from oral tradition.'

'The tradition's died out. We're trying to revive it. The trouble is, they don't know the old stories. Not even *Elf Leyleh wa-Leyleh.*'

'*The Arabian Nights*? Not even that?'

'They rely on old manuscripts, or even fragments of old manuscripts. Many are so tattered and worn that they can't even be read now. My father's been trying to get them together and make a collection of them. We take in old fragments, I copy them, and then we give them back and try to get them into more general circulation.'

'It certainly seems to be livening up the world of story-telling.'

As Katarina did not reply, Owen looked over his shoulder. She was still there.

'Did you come to talk to me about that?' she demanded.

'No. I want to talk about your grandfather.'

'I am with him in everything he does.'

'Should you be?'

Katarina was silent for a moment. Then she said: 'What are you saying?'

'Why is he buying gold?'

'I don't know. Why is he?'

'To buy explosives.'

There was a long silence and again he looked round.

'He knows what he's doing,' she said, a little shakily, however.

'Well, does he? Do you know what explosives do? They blow people up. And not just the people you want to blow up; other people, too. People who are nothing to do with it, children, perhaps. Innocent bystanders who only went there to see the fun.'

'The next alley on the right,' instructed Katarina. 'That is, if you're still insisting.'

'Can't you hear what I'm saying?'

'If you have action to take,' said Katarina, still shaky but determined, 'then take it.'

'I'm trying to prevent the need for action.'

'Why are you talking to me?'

'Because you can stop it.'

'I?' Katarina laughed. 'I?'

'Yes. You. You could persuade him.'

'What makes you think he would listen to me?'

'He loves you.'

'He loves me,' said Katarina, 'but he would not listen.'

'You must try.'

'Must I?' said Katarina. 'You are forgetting: I am with him in everything he does. It was my people they killed. My family that they wiped out.'

'You're the next generation, no, the generation after that, even. It may be right for him to remember but it's not right for you.'

'What do you expect me to do? Betray him?'

'Dissuade him. Stop him from doing something that you know is not right.'

'I don't know it. I don't know what he's doing and I don't care.'

'You must care. There are others to think of as well as him. And I don't mean the Grand Duke. I don't care tuppence about the bloody Grand Duke. But I do care about the others, the ones who have nothing to do with it. And so ought you.'

'I am with my grandfather,' said Katarina obstinately, 'in whatever he does.'

'Think for yourself!'

'I *am* thinking for myself.'

'You're not. You're shut up in that crazy house with him. You listen to him too much. He's sucked you into his crazy dreams. You need to talk to someone else. I wish to hell your father was back here.'

'Do you?' said Katarina, looking at him oddly. 'Do you?'

ᐧᐧᐧ

Sorgos was very pleased to see him.

'You arrive together? Or perhaps...?' Taking in Katarina's slightly flustered state. She immediately disappeared into the recesses of the house.

'Together,' said Owen.

Sorgos led him into what served in that small house as the *mandar'ah*, the reception room and saw him seated on a divan. Then he fussed off calling for Katarina. A little later he returned, carrying a small brazier and lighted coals, which he set down beside Owen.

'I trouble you,' said Owen.

'No trouble at all,' said Sorgos. Katarina came into the room with a brass tray on which there were two little cups, which she put down on a table in front of the divan.

'You are well?'

'Thanks be to God!' Sorgos responded automatically.

'And your granddaughter?'

'Well, too,' Sorgos beamed. 'A beautiful girl, isn't she? And healthy, too. There should be no problem about babies.' His face clouded. 'Only she'll have to get started soon. If she is going to have five.'

'Five?'

'That's what she should be going for. Now, if she had five, and they were all girls, and then each of them had five— why, our problems would be solved in no time at all!'

'I'm not sure you can bank on—'

'Girls are the key, you see. If you want to preserve the language. I've been doing a lot of thinking about this. Language is imbibed with a mother's milk. Men are not so important. Of course, it's a good thing if they have the language, too, but it's not absolutely essential.'

'Perhaps not.'

'Let's face it, there was always a lot of intermarrying among the tribes.'

'Yes, you mentioned the other day that your own wife's father—'

'Just so. The trouble is, the Russians wiped the other tribes out too. About the time that they slaughtered us. So now we have to go further afield.'

The old man looked at Owen hopefully.

'Well, yes, perhaps, um…The Russians have a lot to answer for, don't they?'

'And now is the time when they are going to start answering!' said Sorgos enthusiastically.

'Yes, well, I'm not sure—in fact, that's what I wanted to talk to you about.'

'Going well,' Sorgos assured him.

'Going well?'

'Yes. Fine young men. Plenty of energy. They get on and do things.'

'What sort of things?'

'Assassinating Grand Dukes, for instance.'

This was not quite what Owen wanted to hear.

'Are you sure about this?'

'Oh, quite sure. I was talking it over with them yesterday. Our preparations are well advanced. One or two things still to do, a lot of problem over the—But it will be solved. No, you don't need to worry. We'll be ready when the time comes.'

'I was hoping,' said Owen, 'that you might be having second thoughts.'

'Second thoughts?'

'After the conversation we had the other day.'

'Well, um—what was it exactly that you said?'

'You are not in the Caucasus now. You are in a country to which you owe obligations.'

'Oh, we're not thinking of a general massacre. Just the Grand Duke.'

'It could have international repercussions.'

'You think so?' said Sorgos, pleased.

'I certainly do.'

Sorgos almost rubbed his hands.

'Well, that is excellent!' he said.

'You won't think it so excellent when it rebounds on you.'

'Why should it rebound on us?'

'Do you think Egypt is going to be very pleased?'

'Well…Egypt!'

'Yes, Egypt. A country which has been very generous to you.'

'England will look after Egypt,' said Sorgos confidently. 'Indeed'—his face lit up—'it might turn out to be a very good thing. If we could only provoke a quarrel between England and Russia—! Now, that really would be something! The Grand Duke dead and war as well!'

⚭

'Can we start by getting up to date on the security position?' said Paul. 'Mamur Zapt?'

They were in the committee room again, the one with the trapped flies. But were they the same flies, wondered Owen? Weren't flies supposed to breed quickly and die quickly? Maybe these were the grandchildren of the ones he'd seen the other day. Quick succession of generations. Sorgos would be interested in this.

'Mamur Zapt?' repeated Paul reprovingly.

'Nothing to report.'

'Nothing?'

'Out of the ordinary.'

'No stirrings?'

'The usual.'

It was extraordinarily hot in the room.

'Nothing pertaining to the Grand Duke?'

'I am keeping some people under observation.'

'The Mingrelians?' hazarded the Army major who had been at the meeting the other day.

'Among others.'

'I think this is unsatisfactory,' said Shearer. 'The Mamur Zapt is not being very informative. I can understand his desire to keep intelligence to himself, but we are, surely, a privileged group.'

'Who exactly are the Mingrelians?' asked someone new to the group.

'Troublemakers,' said Shearer.

'Damned difficult lot,' said the major.

'Could drench the city in blood,' said Paul, perking up at the prospect of leading the Army astray.

'My God!' said the newcomer, impressed.

'That's why I'm keeping them under observation,' said Owen helpfully.

'Glad you are. But, um, who—who exactly are they?'

'Slopes of the Caucasus,' said Paul.

'Caucasus?' Shearer sat up. 'Don't like the sound of *that*. Have their links with Russia been explored, sir?'

'Working on it,' said Owen.

'It's not so much links,' said Paul. 'More old enmities. What we're worried about is that some of these may have been carried over to Egypt and may resurface during the Grand Duke's visit.'

'Ah!' said Shearer, leaning forward. 'But is that what we ought to be worried about? I must confess, gentlemen, that I had not appreciated up till now that the Mingrelians and the Russians were neighbours. That makes a big difference.'

'Does it?' said Paul.

'Well, yes, it does. I think we should approach this strategically, gentlemen, and ask what is the Grand Duke's *interest* in coming to Egypt.'

'Well, it's the opera—'

'No, no. no. You misunderstand me. I mean, what is *Russia*'s interest in the Grand Duke's visit?'

'Pretty minimal, I would say.'

'No. No. Its *strategic* interest. From a military point of view.' Shearer looked round the room. 'Perhaps I can help, gentlemen? Bear in mind the location of the Caucasus.'

'The Caucasus? Not too sure,' said the major. 'Up there somewhere?'

'Think of India,' said Shearer, 'and think of the North West Frontier!'

'It's nowhere near the North West Frontier!' said Paul. 'It's the other side of the Caspian Sea!'

'It borders on Persia,' said Owen.

'Exactly!' Shearer turned to him. 'This is where strategic sense is important. Up till now we've assumed that any threat to India would come from the North. That's where we've put our troops. Up on the North West Frontier. But suppose it didn't come from the North. Suppose it came from the West!'

'Persia?'

Shearer nodded.

'Outflanked!' breathed the major. 'Good God!'

'You can see how serious it is,' said Shearer.

'No,' said Paul. 'Nor what it has to do with the Grand Duke's visit.'

'The connection,' said Shearer, 'is Suez. Our main route to India. Cut that and you sever our supply lines.'

'I'm not sure the Grand Duke will be able to do that on his own,' said Owen.

'Of course not!' said Shearer, annoyed. 'Let me take you back to my original question: What is the Grand Duke doing here? What has he *really* come for?

'Well, what *has* he come for?' asked Paul.

'To do a deal,' said Shearer triumphantly. 'A deal with the Khedive. And one that will be in Russia's interests, not ours, I can assure you!'

'Cut the supply lines,' said the major, 'and then strike!'

'Where we least expect it,' said Shearer.

Paul toyed with his pencil.

'You don't see any, well, difficulties with this suggestion?' he said. 'Like having to cross high mountains in winter and then having to cross a neutral country? All before we've noticed it?'

'Don't underestimate the advantages of surprise!' said Shearer.

'Surprising, it would certainly be. Well, thank you, Captain Shearer, for your strategic appraisal. I will certainly see it receives the attention it deserves.'

'Thank you, sir.'

'Meanwhile, perhaps we should return to the point of the present meeting.'

Shearer leaned forward.

'Excuse me, sir, but there is a connection.'

'Yes?'

'The Mingrelians—didn't you say they came from the Caucasus?'

'Well, yes, but—'

'I think we should keep an eye on them. Particularly at the present moment. Some kind of alliance may be in the offing.'

'Between the Russians and the Mingrelians?'

'Exactly!'

'Not from what the Mingrelians were saying yesterday,' said Owen. 'All they seemed to have in mind was killing Russians! Starting with the Grand Duke!'

'I think we must consider the possibility that it's just a blind,' said Shearer.

'Covering what?'

'Their real intentions.'

'Suez,' breathed the major. 'India!'

'We need to ask what they hope to achieve.'

'Well, I can tell you that,' said Owen. 'They hope that by killing the Grand Duke they might be able to provoke a war between England and Russia.'

'Good God!' said the major.

Shearer looked grave.

'Things are more serious than I thought, sir. In fact, I'd almost go so far as to say that we are approaching an emergency situation.'

'You would?' said Paul.

'I would. I think we should review our position very carefully. At the very least we should reappraise our objectives.'

'What had you in mind?' asked Paul. 'Killing the Grand Duke ourselves?'

Chapter 9

The Fustat was not a part of Cairo that Owen was familiar with, so when he received the message from Mahmoud asking him to come urgently to the Fustat police station, he went first to the ferry to get his bearings. Out on the river he could see Roda Island, where, according to tradition, the Arab saint, Moses, was found among the bulrushes. There were not many bulrushes there now. This side of the island consisted mostly of bare, muddy shoals and looked rather like a building site, which, in fact, it was shortly intended to be. At the moment, they were still filling in the land with the debris from collapsed mud houses, quite a lot of which were in the Ders. A long line of camels stretched out across the flimsy wooden footbridge that connected the island to the mainland, each carrying two heavy boxes, one on either side of the hump. Even at this distance he flinched from the smell.

On the other side of the river, beyond the island, he could make out the low houses of the village of Gizeh and behind them, pink in the sun, the pyramids. If you were a tourist you crossed the river higher up, from the modern city. The Babylon ferry was for the humble poor, most of them fellahin going to or coming from the fields on the other side. The ferry was a battered old gyassa, its days of glory on the river now done, sailing, when it was fully loaded, suspiciously low in the water.

Although there were plenty of boats about, gyassas, feluccas and even the occasional dhow, the Old Cairo Landing was not really a port. Vessels bringing grain would go on to Bulaq to unload. Nevertheless, it had something of the air of a dock. There were jetties and mooring posts, boats bobbing on the end of ropes, and, here and there, spindly against the sky, the spars of some larger vessel looming above the houses.

Over to his right was Babylon, but he wasn't going there today. The Fustat police station was in the Arab, not the Coptic, part and inland some way from the ferry.

Mahmoud was sitting in the local Mamur's office. He sprang up as Owen came in and embraced him warmly.

'We've got them all, I think,' he said. 'That little man from the café was very useful. He led us to a café which served as a kind of headquarters for them, or at least a base. I got him to identify as many of the gang as he could. He did very well. He had seen them when they raided Mustapha's. Of course, he's not very keen to give evidence but your man, Selim, will probably do that, won't he?'

'In so far as he can. I don't know at what stage he got hit.'

'The café owner?'

'Mustapha? Hm, I'm not sure…He won't want to stick his neck out. His wife, perhaps.'

'Identification is important,' said Mahmoud sternly. It was one of the crosses he had to bear. Nothing happened unobserved in Cairo; but after the event few would acknowledge that they had seen anything, particularly where a gang was concerned and there was the possibility of reprisals.

'There may be other cafés,' said Owen. 'I'll give you a list. At least of the ones down in the Fustat that have suffered. This gang keeps, I think, to the Fustat for the most part.'

'Yes,' said Mahmoud. 'That's what I wanted to talk to you about. You said you'd like to know who'd commissioned the job at Mustapha's. Well,' he said, 'I think I've found out. Or found out something.'

He went to the door and called out: 'Bring Omar!'

A door slammed somewhere away in the recesses.

'I've been examining them all morning,' said Mahmoud. 'We picked them up last night. This man, Omar, was present when the job was discussed. He says that the gang was approached first through an intermediary and that when they indicated they might be interested, a meeting was arranged with the principal. He was present at that meeting.'

Feet were heard along the corridor. Owen sat down in a chair over to one side of the room, where he could watch Omar but would not interfere. This, now, was Mahmoud's case.

Mahmoud made a sign to the two constables and they stepped back.

'Well, Omar,' said Mahmoud pleasantly; 'just a few questions. Nothing new, just going over ground we've covered. I want to make sure I've got it right. This job, now, at Mustapha's: out of the usual run for you, I think you said?'

'That's right. And I wish we'd never heard of it.'

'You should have stuck to the Fustat.'

'We should. I said that at the time. Stick to what we know, I said. I mean, we weren't even getting any money out of it!'

'Not getting any money? But, Omar, you were hoping to get money, surely? Why else were you working the café?'

'We were doing it for someone else. *We* weren't making any money. It was all going to go to him!'

'But, Omar, if it was all going to go to him, what was there in it for you?'

'Well, that's what I said. Only Narouz said, "We're doing this as a favour. It's exceptional, see?" And I said, "Well, I don't see. Why should we be doing anybody a favour?" And he said: "Because we owe Hussein al-Fadal one, that's why, and Hussein is not the sort you don't pay back when you're asked." Well, I knew about Hussein, of course, everybody knows about Hussein, and I wasn't going to argue too much, not with Hussein. So I went along with it. But it was a mistake. I know we didn't have much choice, you've got to do people a favour when you owe one, but it was a mistake all the same. Look where it's got us!'

'Let's get this straight: you were going to squeeze money out of Mustapha and then give it to—?'

'Hussein's friend. Don't ask me why. Maybe Hussein owed *him* a favour.'

'Can you tell me about this friend?'

'Well, yes, I certainly don't owe *him* a favour. We met him at Ali's. It's a little coffee house not far from the ferry. It was all set up, really. I mean, there wasn't any bargaining about terms. He knew that we were going to do what he asked. All he had to do was tell us what he wanted.'

'And what did he want?'

'Just to call on Mustapha and get the money.'

'Have you any idea why it was Mustapha you were to call on? Was there anything special about him?'

'I don't think so. I think he had just seen this place and thought it would be a good one to call on. The important thing was the money. He wanted it quick. I said: "Why don't you break in somewhere and steal it?" But he said no, that wouldn't do, protection was easier. And then he named the sum he wanted. I said: "That's ridiculous!" And he said: "That's what I want." And I said: "Look, you're not going about it in the right way. A little at a time but lots of times, that's what you want. It makes it easier for everyone." But he said no, he needed the money now. It had to be upfront in a lump sum. Well, it didn't matter to us, it was easier in a way because it meant we only had to do the café once. But it was a bit odd, if you know what I mean. It's not the way you usually go about business like this, not the way we do it, at any rate. It's sort of, well, amateur.'

'But that's what he wanted?'

'That's what he wanted, so that's what he got. Or would have got.'

'What sort of man was he?'

'Ah, well, now, I'm not sure. I...well, that would be telling, wouldn't it?'

'You could tell me a bit. After all, you don't owe him anything. It's the other way round if anything. He owes *you* something.'

'Well, maybe. But I don't know that I could tell you much, anyway. I only saw him the once.'

'But you saw him. So what sort of man was he?'

'Well, he wasn't an Arab, for a start. That's another thing I didn't like. "Let's stick to our own," I said. "Then we know where we are."'

'A Copt, was he?'

'Oh, no, no. Not as bad as that.' He hesitated. 'I don't know what he was, really. But Sayeed—he was with me—said that he thought he was one of those funny people, Christians, you know, thin faces, dark hair—'

'Armenians?'

'No, no. The other side of Turkey.'

'Georgians?' said Mahmoud.

∽∾

They took Omar to the Der. He looked around him uneasily.

'Don't like these places much,' he said.

'Keep your galabeeyah over your face,' advised Mahmoud. 'Then no one will recognize you.'

'It's not that,' said Omar. 'It's the place. All tunnels. All darkness. Like being in a grave.'

Al-Mo'allaka was dark, too. The lamps had been turned down and the air was dense with incense. In one corner there was a small light where the man was working. They went across.

'I come again,' said Owen. 'I have brought someone who would like to see your work.'

The man bowed acknowledgement, then lifted the lamp so that Mahmoud could see the ikon better. The gold seemed to stand out in the darkness, to glow with a deep, remarkable light. Mahmoud examined it attentively.

'This, here...' he said, pointing.

The workman peered at the spot. His face showed clear in the light of the lamp.

Owen, holding on to Omar, felt him shake his head.

They went downstairs to the workshop.

'Still at it?' said Owen.

'For another week,' said the workman.

Mahmoud picked up a piece of board with paint on it and stepped out into the sunlight to see it better.

The workman looked up.

'Just trying out the colours,' he said. 'You've got to get them right.'

'How do you get this?' said Mahmoud, pointing.

The man went over to stand beside him. Again, Owen felt Omar shake his head.

As they came out, Georgiades materialized beside them.

'A leather-worker's next,' he said. They followed him through a forest of arches and then into an inner courtyard. Along one wall there was another series of arches, each of which held a small workshop. Several of them were tailors. They sat on the broad counter of their shop sewing by hand. Another was heavy with the smell of spices. As they came to the one at the end there was the smell of burnt leather. Two men were busy at a fire at the back. They looked up as Mahmoud went in. Omar shook his head.

Georgiades led them on.

Towards the end of the morning Owen began to feel that it was a long time since he had seen the sunlight. He sometimes felt like that in the Bab-el-Khalk but there, although the shutters were closed against the heat, the darkness was never quite as absolute and oppressive as it was here. Everyone worked by lamplight. It was as if they were all moles inhabiting some underground gallery.

Omar shook his head to all the Georgians he was shown. Owen began to wonder if this was not after all a wild goose chase, if he had brought Mahmoud and Omar here in pursuit of a mere chimera of coincidence.

Georgiades stopped.

'What's this?'

'A bookbinder's. It used to be Sorgos's.' He looked at Owen. 'I think you'd better stay outside,' he said.

Owen shrugged and watched Mahmoud go in with Omar.

'Why do I have to stay outside?'

'Because the person in there might recognize you. And wonder.'

It was some little time before the two came out.

'Interesting books,' said Mahmoud. 'They do a lot of work for the Law School Library.'

They walked on round a corner and then up some steps and then, to his surprise, Owen found himself high up on one of the old Roman walls of the fortress and looking down on the small courtyard of the Mo'allaka.

'Well?' said Owen.

Mahmoud nodded.

'Djugashvili,' he said.

ᏯᎷᎧ

On his way back to the Bab-el-Khalk, cutting through side streets, Owen came upon a riot. The street was jammed with people shaking their fists and shouting. There was a crash of collapsing stalls, agitated shouts, accompanied, strangely enough, by bleating. Two sheep shot out from under the feet of the crowd and ran off distractedly down the road. More agitated shouts and then a small boy shot likewise from under the feet of the crowd and ran off in pursuit. More splintering of woodwork and now some things were being thrown. Small objects, stones? Already red.

Owen came to a halt. He had thought at first that this was merely an ordinary traffic dispute, caused, say, by a man carrying a bed on a donkey, the donkey, small, the bed big and lying flat on the donkey's back, the ends protruding across the street, the man, again, big, sitting on top of the bed, meeting, say, a forage camel, grumpy, huge loads of berseem slung on either side of its back, so huge that they, too, spread out across the street, both animals unwieldy and neither driver able, or inclined, to go back, the exchange of insults egged on by admiring onlookers, developing partisanship and, in no time at all, tumult. Despite the ferocity of the rhetoric and the postures that the would-be combatants took up, such things usually sorted themselves out peacefully when everybody had had their fun. But this looked different. The blood—

Or was it blood? And were the missiles stones? Or were they—yes, tomatoes! From the upset stall, perhaps. Thrown in rage—was that right?—by the offended stall owner? What *was* all this about?

At the heart of the dispute there appeared to be two men, held back by supporters but straining to throw themselves on each other, insults streaming through foaming lips.

Owen pushed his way through the throng and came out beside them. He found himself in front of an Arab coffee house, the owner of which, his face perspiring profusely, was trying desperately to pacify the two men.

'What is all this?' said Owen sternly.

The proprietor grabbed at him with relief.

'Effendi! Oh, Effendi, these two men—!'

Owen turned on them.

'Stop that!' he barked. 'Any more nonsense from you and you'll be in the caracol!'

One of them quietened down. The other went on shouting. Owen caught him by the folds of his galabeeyah.

'Did you hear me?' he said threateningly. 'I said quieten down!'

He lifted the man up on to his toes and shook him.

'That's better.' He released the man. 'Now, what's all this about?'

The crowd calmed down. The proprietor pushed forward.

'Effendi, these two men—scoundrels, rascals, vagabonds! They started it.'

The two men turned on him in unison.

'Liar! Thief! *You* started it!'

'*I* started it?' said the proprietor, stepping back hurriedly.

'Yes, you started it. Everything was all right until you started mucking about!'

'Well, I wouldn't say that—' began the other man.

'I just thought it was time for a change, that's all!' said the proprietor, sweating.

'Well, you've got change, haven't you?' said one of the protagonists belligerently. 'Him, or me?'

'Isn't that enough?' demanded the other man.

'Well, no. It's either him or it's you. Either Abu Zeyd or Sultan Baybars.'

Owen saw now that both men were storytellers.

'What's wrong with that?'

'I'm *telling* you. People would like a change.'

'In the stories of Abu Zeyd there is inexhaustible variety.'

'Well, not quite inexhaustible—'

'I see what you mean,' said the other man swiftly. 'They are a bit the same. Whereas the stories of Sultan Baybars—'

'We've heard them all before,' said the proprietor, wiping his face. 'We want new ones.'

'New ones!'

'Well, yes, new ones. Now, this new fellow—'

'A charlatan!'

'A fake!'

'No art!'

'No feeling!'

'Yes, but they're new. We've not heard the stories before. He's got a bit of imagination, this bloke has.'

'Imagination!'

'You don't want imagination. What you want is tradition. You want to know where you are.'

'Isn't there room for you all?' asked Owen. 'One of you one day, the other the next?'

'Ah, that's how it starts. But then you get somebody else in, and then another, and before you know where you are, your livelihood's gone. You've got to make a stand!'

'There's too many coming into the profession, if you ask me. Every time you go to a café these days you've got competition.'

'And it's not from people you know, it's from these new men!'

'Upstarts!'

'No tradition!'

'No training!'

'Stories from the gutter!'

'They undermine the dignity of the profession!'

'Dignity!' said the proprietor. 'You lot?'

☙

'One day, Rice Pudding went up on to the roof to hang out the washing and when she had finished, she sat down among the bean plants to rest from her labours. Fancying herself concealed, she took off her veil to cool her face. Now it so happened that in the house next to hers, there lived a handsome youth who, that very afternoon, had gone up on to the roof to air himself among the tomato plants and cucumber flowers and melons. He should have been happy but he was sad at heart. He took two melons in his hands.'

'"Alas," he said, "these are warm and round and inviting as the breasts of a beautiful maiden. But where is there a beautiful maiden for me?"'

'At that very moment he looked across the roof and saw Rice Pudding sitting in her bower.'

'He let the melons fall.

'"Light of my life!" he said. "Delight of my days! Hope of my heart! Dream of my dreams!"

'Unfortunately, in his ecstasy, he spoke so loudly that Rice Pudding heard him and took fright.

'"You have seen what you should not have seen," she said, and ran back down below.

'Every day after that the youth went up on to the roof and hid among the tomato plants and hoped that Rice Pudding would come again. For many days she did not but then one day, when it was very hot, she said to herself. "Oh, how I would like to cool my face! Surely, if I sit among the bean plants he will not see me?"'

'These women!' said Selim from the doorway. 'Talk themselves into anything!'

Some women in the crowd hushed him indignantly. The storyteller gave him a cold look and then went on:

'So she went up on to the roof and sat among the bean flowers. And after a while she took off her veil. The youth could not contain himself.

'"Flower among the flowers!" he called. "Beauty among the beautiful! Bestow the brilliance of your eyes upon him who worships you!"

'Rice Pudding started up with surprise.'

'Oh, yes?' said Selim. 'I'll bet!'

The storyteller paused ostentatiously but then allowed himself to be persuaded to continue.

'"What is this?" she said. "A man's voice? A man's eyes!"

'And she made to rush from the roof.

'"Stay!" cried the youth. "Oh, stay! Heart of my heart, take not your light from me! All I ask is permission to woo thee honourably!"

'"Alas!" said Rice Pudding. "That can never be!"

'"My house is honourable, my family rich. How, then, can your father object?"

'"It is not that," said Rice Pudding sadly. "It is not that."'

The repetition, delivered in a faltering cadence, was felt by his audience to be a fine touch. It murmured appreciatively. Even Selim was impressed.

"'What then can it be?'

"'I have lost,' said Rice Pudding, "that which I would have kept.'"

'Already?' said Selim, aghast. 'The bitch!'

"'My name,' said Rice Pudding, "has been taken from me."

"'Your good name? But—?'

"'*Not* my good name,' said Rice Pudding, a little crossly. "My name. My actual name. It ran away."

"'I am bemused,' said the youth.

"'Well, that is understandable,' said Rice Pudding kindly. "But you can see the difficulty."

"'If that is all,' said the youth, recovering, "then it is nothing. I will go out and find the name. And when I find it, I will return it to you. What is yours will be yours. But after that I shall marry you. And then what is yours will be mine."'

'Oh, very good!' said Selim, applauding vigorously. The crowd, too, was much taken by the rhetorical inversions.

The storyteller bowed acknowledgement, got up off the mastaba, and sent a boy round with the bowl.

'Tell me, Mustapha,' said Owen, sipping his coffee, 'how did you come to get a storyteller such as this? For he is neither an Abu Zeyd man nor a Sultan Baybars man.'

'He's all right, isn't he? Good for business. A bit different.'

'How did you come by him?'

'Well, I was sitting in here one day when a man came in, an effendi, like yourself. At that time I had one of the old storytellers, an Abu Zeyd man, I think he was. Well, this effendi listened to his story and afterwards he beckoned me over.

"'A café like this which is going somewhere," he said, "needs something a bit different. Have you ever thought of getting a new storyteller?" "Well," I said, "they're all the same, really, aren't they? The stories are all the same and they don't amount to much. To tell the truth, I hardly listen to them nowadays." "That's just the point," he said. "You don't listen to them and nor does anybody else. They're hardly a draw, are they? Now suppose you got somebody telling new stories; they'd come and listen to him, wouldn't they?" "Well, they might," I said, "but really what they come here for is coffee and a bit of chat, a bit of company, you know, and a breath of cool air."

'Well, he laughed at that. "All the same," he said, "you could do with a new attraction. Bring in one or two more." Well, you know, there was something in what he said. Business builds up for a bit, you know, and then it stagnates. "I could put you in touch with someone," he said. "Abdul Hosein wouldn't like that," I said—Abdul was the storyteller I had at the time, the one that we'd just been listening to. "Whose money are we talking about?" he said. "His or yours?"'

'And so Abdul Hosein went?' said Owen.

'He certainly did. Kicked up a bit of a fuss about it. Said he had friends who wouldn't like it. I mentioned that to the new storyteller. "I've got friends, too," he said, and smiled. "Yes," I said, "but how many? He's an Abu Zeyd man and there're a lot of them." "There's a lot of me, too," he said. "We're a new lot. We're growing fast. You don't want to get stuck with the old lot, not now, when the competition's hotting up." He had something there. Anyway, I kept him on.'

'This effendi, what sort of man was he?'

'Small, very polite.'

'English?'

'No, no.' Mustapha hesitated. 'It's hard to say. None of the usual ones. Not Greek. Not Turk. Somewhere over there, though.'

Owen guessed he was hearing about Katarina's father. He had hitherto, without thinking about it, put him down as a bookish man. Sorgos had given the impression that he lacked spirit. Was it just that his spirit expressed itself in ways other than the old man's nationalism?

⎯⎯⎯

'Djugashvili,' said Georgiades. 'Friend of Sorgos, friend of the man working on the ikons, friend of quite a lot of people down in the Der. Came to Cairo only six years ago. Left Georgia in a hurry after some trouble with the Russians.'

'What was the trouble?'

'I don't know exactly. There was a sort of Nationalist movement, anti-Russian, of course, and he was involved. How far it got, I don't know, but he's much admired, down in the Der, as a man of action.'

'Sorgos likes men of action,' said Owen.

⎯⎯⎯

'They need money,' said Nikos. 'That's it, isn't it? We know they were having difficulty in finding it—Nicodemus said so. Well, time is running out. They've got to find it quickly. So they've had to turn to this.'

'Commissioning a gang to get it for them?'

'Why not? We've said all along they're amateurs. It's the first time they've done anything like this. Want money? How about a spot of protection? Don't know how to go about it? How about someone who does?'

'And you find someone near to you, a gang in the Fustat, and you approach them through an intermediary because you don't know any gangs yourself. I can see all that: but what I don't see is how they are paying for it. If it's with money, that destroys the object.'

'Favours. The world runs on favours. Especially the Arab world.'

'The gang owes this fellow Hussein a favour, OK, and that's why they're doing it. But what is Hussein getting? What can Sorgos and the others give him?'

'Maybe they don't have to give him anything. Maybe he's returning a favour too.'

'And they're just calling it in?'

'That's right. They're owed the favour and they're exchanging it for cash. This way.'

'It's possible,' said Owen, 'but—'

'What's wrong?'

'Why do they have to do it this way? Why go in for all the complication? Why do they have to use explosives? Why not use a bullet? It would be much simpler.'

Nikos and Georgiades looked at each other. Both shrugged.

'Does it matter?' asked Georgiades. 'So long as that's the way they *are* doing it.'

'No,' Owen admitted.

'That certainly seems the way they're committed to,' said Nikos. 'Sorgos is still rushing around desperately trying to buy gold and the only reason I can see for that is that it's crucial to them if they want to get their hands on the explosives in time.'

'No money,' said Georgiades, 'no explosives!'

'That being so,' said Nikos, 'isn't the next step obvious?'

Chapter 10

'My young friend from the mountains!' cried Sorgos.

'Not this time,' said Owen; 'the Mamur Zapt.'

Sorgos's smile disappeared.

'So,' he said. 'It has come. I had hoped—But never mind. You have your duty to do. Well, do it.'

He held out his hands.

'Not yet,' said Owen. 'Let us talk. It may not be necessary.'

He followed Sorgos into the small room.

'Well?' said Sorgos, turning and facing him.

'I had hoped you would have heard my words,' said Owen. 'You are in a country which has treated you with honour and justice. I had hoped you would respond likewise.'

Sorgos drew himself up. His eyes flashed.

'Do you accuse me of not behaving with honour?'

'What you are to yourself cannot be separated from what you are to the country you have come to.'

'What I owe to myself is a private matter!' said Sorgos furiously.

'If you were a guest in a man's house, and your enemy came to that house and was also received as a guest, would you offend your host's kindness?'

'I would wait until my enemy left before killing him.'

'Then do the same here, where you are also a guest.'

'Do you think I have not thought of that?'

'I think you have not thought of that enough.'

'It is not just I,' said Sorgos, not giving an inch; 'it is my people.'

'The Mingrelians? Does not what I have said apply to them, too? Are they not also guests?'

'We have suffered,' said Sorgos, breathing heavily, 'and we will be revenged.'

'Is that what Mingrelians do,' asked Owen, 'offend their host?'

'They kill their enemies,' said Sorgos fiercely.

'Anywhere? In the house of another, so that the blame will fall on them? Can this be honour?'

Sorgos was for a moment at a loss.

'This, too, is a country. Here, too, are a people,' said Owen, pressing home his advantage. 'Why should they suffer because of a cause which is not theirs?'

'It *is* theirs,' said Sorgos fiercely. 'It is every man's cause. Why should the poor, the small, the weak be trodden down by the mighty? It is not Russia that we are resisting but oppression!'

'A man must choose his cause,' said Owen, 'and you must let them choose theirs.'

'I had hoped,' said Sorgos, 'that you, as a man from the mountains, would understand.'

'I do understand. It is because I come from a country like yours, small, like yours, proud, like yours, that my heart goes out to you. We, too, have been invaded, oppressed, for much longer than you have, for many centuries. And from the centuries we have learned a lesson: that death breeds death. For a people to live there must be an end to the killing.'

'They took away our country,' said Sorgos. 'They did not take away yours. For a people to live, they must have a land. When even that is taken away, all you are left with is the spirit. In time even that will fade. The young—I must not say that, Katarina says I must not say that, that the young have always been like this but that somehow they grow up and then are like the old. That they will care as I do and fight as I do. But,' said Sorgos, 'I fear—'

'It is for them to choose,' said Owen, 'not for you.'

'I am the last,' said Sorgos. 'In my heart I know it. I had hoped to rebuild a people but they turn their backs on me. Even my granddaughter does not understand when I say that there must be children. The time is coming when the Mingrelians will be no more. Well, so let it be. But if it has to end, let it end with honour. I will kill the Grand Duke.'

'I had hoped to persuade you otherwise.'

'You mean well,' said Sorgos, 'but you come too late.'

'I do not think so. Where is the gold?'

'The gold?' said Sorgos, starting back.

Owen went to the door and threw it open. The men began to file in.

'Here is my search warrant,' he said, pulling it out of his pocket and showing it to Sorgos.

'Katarina!' cried the old man.

Owen ran out. She was not in any of the rooms at the back, nor in any of those upstairs. He ran out into a small yard at the back of the house in which clothes were hanging up to dry. From one side of the yard a flight of steps ran up to the roof. Owen raced up them.

Katarina was bending over a pile of brushwood. As with many of the houses, the roof was used not just for sleeping on in hot weather but also for storing fuel and vegetables.

Owen kicked the wood aside. Beneath, was a pile of onions. He kicked these aside too. They were covering a drain. He lifted the lid and felt inside. A bag, very heavy, and then a second one. He lifted them out.

'You were very quick,' he said, looking up at Katarina.

'I was listening,' she said.

He carried the bags downstairs.

'All right,' he said, and the men stopped searching. 'You can go now.'

They all filed out.

'Do you want me as well?' said Katarina, flushed and angry.

'You are with him in everything. Yes, I know. Even when it comes to blowing up innocent people with explosives. No, I don't want you. I don't even, as a matter of fact, want him.'

'I am ready,' said Sorgos fiercely.

'You stay here. For the time being.'

'You are not arresting me?'

Sorgos seemed bewildered.

'No. And I hope now that I will never need to.'

'But—?'

Katarina suddenly understood.

'He has not come for you,' she said.

'But then—? What have you come for?'

Owen picked up the bags of gold dust.

'You can have them back,' he said. 'After.'

⚭

'Why didn't you arrest him while you were at it?' said Georgiades.

'There's still time for them to change their plans. They could still try a bullet. I want him free so that he can run around and talk to the other people. Then we can pick them up.'

'They're not going to be as naïve as that,' said Nikos doubtfully.

'You've been saying how naïve they are. A bunch of amateurs. Well, we'll see. Anyway,' said Owen with satisfaction, 'I reckon we've put a spoke in their wheel.'

'No gold, no explosives!' said Georgiades. 'Neat!'

'It's nicer to do it this way,' said Owen, 'if we can.'

He looked round the table.

'Right, now let's look at preparations for the visit generally: how are things going? Nikos?'

Nikos spread out his papers.

'And now,' said Paul, settling himself into his chair, 'about the preparations for the Grand Duke's visit: how are things going? His Highness arrives at Alexandria this afternoon and transfers to the Khedivial Yacht tomorrow morning. Now, is everything in hand? Mamur Zapt?'

'No reports of intended action. Except, of course, for our Mingrelian friends, and there, I hope, we have been able to take preventive measures.'

'Good. Any feel for the popular mood?'

'Indifferent.'

'Welcoming,' put in the Khedive's representative hastily. 'Eager anticipation.'

'Oh, good. That will be very important when we come to the procession. But that, of course, is near the end of the visit. Let's take it in order. First, the Khedivial Yacht and the journey through the Suez Canal—'

The meeting droned on. The flies dipped in sympathy. Had they fallen asleep, Owen wondered. Now, that was interesting. Were committee meetings so boring that even the flies fell asleep? Could you use the flies as a measure of the boringness of a committee? You could release, say, six flies at the start of a committee and see at what point they all sank soporifically down. You could even measure rates. If they all sank down pretty soon after the start of the meeting, God, that was a hell of a meeting—

'Captain Shearer?'

'I think I can confidently say, gentlemen,' concluded Shearer, 'that all preparations are now complete and that the Army is ready for all contingencies.'

'Hear, hear!' said the major.

'Including explosives?' asked Owen.

'Explosives? Well—'

'Bloody hell!' said the major.

'Depends how they're used,' said Shearer, frowning. 'We'll
line the streets during the procession and keep people well
back, beyond throwing distance—'

'Suppose they're buried or hidden in a building? A large
cache?'

'A mine, you mean?' said the major, disturbed.

'That sort of thing.'

'Well, it would be difficult to guard against all eventu-
alities,' said Shearer, less confidently. 'I mean, we'd have to
check all the buildings beforehand—'

'*All* the buildings?' asked Paul. 'I'm a bit worried about
the practicalities of this.'

'We'd have to get in some extra men, of course. There's a
battalion of British troops at Aden, and there may be just
time to ask India—'

'It would look bad,' said Paul. 'It would suggest we couldn't
cope with things ourselves.'

'We can handle it,' said Shearer automatically. 'We can
handle it.'

'Are you sure?' asked Paul.

'We'll need sappers,' said the major worriedly. 'Mines are
damned nasty things.'

'How serious a possibility is this?' asked Paul, looking at
Owen.

'Oh, a definite possibility. We've heard that some explosives, possibly connected to the visit of the Grand Duke, are
coming in at Suez.'

'My God!' breathed the major.

'We'll do all we can to intercept them, of course,' said
Owen, 'but I can't guarantee anything. There's too much
coming into Suez for us to be able to search everything. I
have to say that it remains a possibility, a distinct possibility.
Thought you'd like to know,' he said sweetly to Shearer, 'since
you'll be taking responsibility for the procession.'

'What's this?' said Paul.

'Captain Shearer and I have agreed. He is assuming full responsibility for the procession. Unified policing,' said Owen innocently.

༺ ༻

Paul had been trying to catch his eye, and when the meeting was over and the Army had departed he came up to him.

'Now, look,' he said, '*I'm* in that procession—'

'It'll be all right,' Owen assured him hastily. 'It's not as bad as that. I think I've put a spoke in that particular wheel. But I just thought it might give Shearer a sleepless night or two.'

'Perhaps I could get the Old Man to travel at the front of the procession instead,' said Paul thoughtfully.

༺ ༻

Owen was meeting Zeinab for lunch after the meeting and he suggested that Paul should come along.

'An apéritif, perhaps,' said Paul, glancing at his watch. 'I'll tell her about the arrangements I've been making for the Grand Duke's visit.'

'Paul, I don't think she's that interested—'

'She will be in what I have to tell her,' said Paul confidently. 'It's about the opera. Now, I've really been giving my mind to this. It's our one chance to get something out of this damned visit so we must take it. I've been saying to everyone that we've simply got to have an opera or the visit won't be a true replica of the previous one. I know that in fact they didn't actually get to see an opera, but the point is they *would* have seen one if it had been ready. It was there *in spirit*. That's what I told the Khedive yesterday, anyway, and he agreed. He likes the colour and the clothes and the pretty women. Oh, and the music, too. Anyway, he's agreed.'

'Wonderful! But, Paul, surely there won't be time to—'

'Oh, it won't be a completely new production. There isn't time for that. It'll have to be one they've got in repertoire, but that's *La Bohème*, so that's all right. Zeinab will like that. She always identifies with Mimi. Now my idea is this: we can't change the opera but we can change the singers. Or at least some of them. So why not get in somebody special? Fonseca and Peppone, say. There's still time for them to get here from Italy. Somebody special for a special occasion, I said to the Khedive. He liked that.'

'It'll cost millions!'

'Yes, but Finance won't find out until it's all over. That's the beauty of it, you see.'

'Well, I do see, but—'

'I can't wait to tell Zeinab.'

The Ismailiya, where Owen was meeting Zeinab, was the modern European quarter of Cairo. There were the business houses, banks and consulates; there, too, the hotels and fashionable shops, the salons and the French-style cafés. No storytellers outside them! And there was Zeinab, dressed à la Parisienne, conceding so much to Egypt as to wear a veil, but not so much as for it to be one that would be a *soupçon* out of place on the Faubourg St Honoré.

On hearing Paul's news about the opera she went straight for the jugular.

'So,' she said, 'two dresses, not one. That makes it even more impossible. There's still time. Are you going to send the cable or not?'

'Not,' said Owen firmly.

'Cable?' said Paul. 'What cable?'

'To her couturier. In Paris. By the Diplomatic Postbag.'

'Why not?' said Paul.

'There you are!' said Zeinab triumphantly. 'Why not?'

'Because it's a misuse of public funds. Why can't she use the Post and Telegraphs like everyone else?'

Zeinab put her hand on Paul's.

'He is a simple man,' she said. 'He does not understand these things. But you understand them, don't you? You understand that there are some things a woman might wish to keep secret from other women until the right moment, the moment of éclat, that she might not wish to blazon her secrets through all Cairo by using the public Post Office?'

'You overrate the interest of all Cairo in what you are going to wear.'

'Overrate?' said Zeinab pityingly. 'When the British ladies talk of nothing else? Samira was at the hairdresser's with the Consul-General's wife yesterday and she said that all the talk was of what everyone was going to wear. Samira herself—'

'I do think she has a point, you know,' Paul said to Owen. 'I was talking to the C-G's wife only this morning—'

Zeinab patted his hand.

'You understand,' she purred, 'because you have imagination.'

'Gosh, yes!' said Paul.

'Paul, she's eating you alive!'

'*He* has no imagination,' said Zeinab pointedly. 'That is because he is British. They have it cut out of them in childhood. Like tonsils.'

'*I'm* British,' said Paul faintly.

'But you are different, Paul. You *have* imagination. And sensitivity. You understand women.'

'If he doesn't,' said Owen, 'he's getting a pretty good lesson.'

Zeinab gave him a black look.

'The cable needs to go off today,' she said.

'Look,' said Paul, 'if it matters that much, why don't I send it?'

'There!' said Zeinab, looking at Owen.

'No!' said Owen.

'I'd be glad to, honestly!' said Paul.

'That's not the point,' said Owen.

'No,' agreed Zeinab, 'that's not the point.'

'I don't understand,' said Paul, bewildered.

'*I've* got to send it,' said Owen.

'That's right,' said Zeinab.

'I don't—'

'It's nothing to do with dresses,' said Owen. 'She doesn't care a damn about that sort of thing. It's to do with her and me.'

'Quite right,' said Zeinab.

'I'm out of my depth,' said Paul.

'She wants to show her power over me.'

'What nonsense!' said Zeinab. 'I want *you* to show your love for me.'

'I'm backing out,' said Paul, quickly finishing his apéritif.

Owen looked at Zeinab.

'It's all right,' he said. 'It's all over.'

'That's right,' agreed Zeinab picking up the menu. 'What's for lunch?'

'Someone else, I hope,' said Paul, rising from his chair.

⌘

The chandeliers glittered. Ice tinkled in the glasses. Redsashed suffragis bowed. A small group of men entered the room and began to move round the guests.

'Prince Oblomov,' introduced the nervous young member of the Chargé's staff; 'Captain—' He looked down at his prompt card and swallowed.

'Cadwallader,' said McPhee quickly, anxious to be helpful. 'Cadwallader Owen.'

It was McPhee who had prepared the prompt list. Hence the inclusion of the Cadwallader. The name was a secret that Owen preferred to keep. He had, however, once made the mistake of signing his name in full in McPhee's presence and McPhee, a Celt himself and a romantic, had never forgotten.

'I beg your pardon?' said the Prince.

'Cadwallader. It's an ancient Welsh name, the name of the Welsh ruling family, in fact—'

'Ah!' said the Prince, interested, and turning to Owen. 'You are a member of the Royal Family?'

'No, no!' said Owen hastily, cursing McPhee. 'It's just a name. Not uncommon in Wales. My mother—'

'I quite understand,' said the Prince sympathetically. 'I'm illegitimate myself. Or so they say.'

'No, no. It was just that my mother fancied there was a remote family connection and, being a bit of a romantic—'

'Quite,' said the Prince. 'Always giving her heart away. I'm like that too. A bit of a romantic.'

'What's all this?' asked the Russian Chargé, joining the group.

'I was explaining about Owen's name,' said McPhee.

'Gareth?' said the Chargé, who knew Owen well.

'No, Cadwallader.'

'Just a minute,' said the Prince. 'What *is* his name?'

'Owen,' said Owen.

'Gareth Cadwallader,' supplemented McPhee. 'Gareth is the Christian, or first name; Cadwallader the second, or middle—'

The Prince looked at the Chargé desperately.

'My name is Ivan Stepanovich,' said the Chargé cheerfully, 'if that helps. Oh, and Volkonsky, too, of course.'

'I thought it might interest the Prince,' said McPhee, perspiring slightly, 'because of the Welsh connection.'

'Welsh? Oh, yes. Like those soldiers, you mean? Prince, I hope His Royal Highness hasn't forgotten about them. I mentioned them in my communiqué, if you remember.'

'A decoration, was that it?' said the Prince vaguely.

'For services rendered. Against our Mingrelian adversaries.'

'In battle, was it?'

'Yes. You could say that. Pretty well.'

'Oh, there'll be no problem. His Royal Highness will be only too glad to, I'm sure. I'll have a word with him when he arrives. Most appropriate. In view of the British, er, presence… Well, I'm very pleased to have met you, Captain Cadwallader Gareth.'

ᘓᙏᙏᙎ

'Guard of Honour? The Fusiliers? Not their turn,' said the Army.

'You don't think the Sirdar could stretch a point? In view of them being especially singled out?'

❧

'Thank you very much, sir,' said the Welsh Fusiliers doubtfully when Owen came across them that evening as they were making for the Ezbekiyeh. 'But if it's all the same to you, we'd rather not. It's going to be that hot standing out there in the sun …'

'The DCLI, perhaps?' suggested Owen.

'Oh, sir, that would be wonderful. Give those bastards a taste of something.'

'I'll see what I can do. The Army wasn't all that keen on you lot, anyway.'

'Any chance of us being on guard at the Opera House, sir? I mean, he's going there, isn't he? It's a special night. They're getting some Italian singers…there's a very good tenor, they say …'

❧

'It's ridiculous!' complained Mahmoud. 'The city is going crazy about him. They're getting all the bunting out, putting flags up everywhere…and who is he? Just some petty Russian aristocrat. Why is he getting this treatment? It's demeaning. The Khedive is demeaning himself…other countries will think we're glad to get anyone!'

'Don't make too much of it!' Owen advised. 'It's some kind of recognition, isn't it?'

'Is it?' said Mahmoud. 'Who is being recognized? The Khedive? The British? Not Egypt. Is he going to talk to anybody who's been democratically elected? Is there going to be any discussion of the Capitulations? Of the British presence? Is he going to address the National Assembly?'

'From what I hear,' said Owen, 'he couldn't even address an envelope.'

'They're sending a cipher,' complained Mahmoud. 'That's not recognition; that's insult!'

'It's something,' said Owen pacifically, 'some kind of diplomatic recognition. And that's better than nothing.'

Mahmoud snorted.

'It's a waste of money,' he said. 'Money that could be used to do a lot of good: build houses, build hospitals, improve maternity care, education, sewage——' He made a gesture of hopelessness. 'There's so much to do,' he said bitterly, 'and we're spending our time on this!'

'I know!' said Owen soothingly. 'When we could be getting on with our jobs!'

Mahmoud, however, the Nationalist bit between his teeth, was not to be soothed.

'And that's another thing!' he said fiercely. 'I had hoped that the visit might give us an opportunity to raise that internationally!'

'What?'

'Policing. Law and order. Who should be responsible, Britain or Egypt? And why isn't the British Army subject to Egyptian law?'

'I don't think that question is on the agenda.'

'I'll bet it isn't! And none of the real questions are, are they? They're all being kept out of the way, just as we, the Egyptians, are being kept out of the way. Well, one day, I can tell you, we won't be kept out of the way, we won't allow ourselves to be managed aside. We shall strike back!'

Owen, however, declined to be stirred. He was feeling relaxed now that all the preparations were complete. All was under control.

'Not until the Grand Duke's visit is over, I hope,' he said benignly.

⁊⊶⊷⊷⊷⊶

Once Mahmoud had got his teeth into something, he did not let go; and since the arrest of the gang he had been biting hard in the Fustat. On the fringes of the gang there were the usual supporters, friends and accomplices and one by one he

had been pulling them in, making the most of this opportunity to clean up the criminal quarter around the Old Docks.
One of the names mentioned by Omar, the man they had
questioned together, had been that of Hussein al-Fadal, and
Mahmoud had been giving him some attention.

'He's tough, all right. He works a fleet of boats out of the
Old Docks. They go right up beyond Luxor, fuel and grain,
mostly, though some stone from the quarries. In his father's
time they went further still, beyond Khartoum. It was said
he used to bring back slaves. A tough old man and a tough
son. I suppose you have to be, working on the river.
Anyway—this is the point that will interest you—the father
is not a native Egyptian. He comes from one of those countries up around the Caucasus, Muslim, so there was no great
difficulty about settling here. The story goes that he was
driven out by the Russians. That would have been about the
time that Sorgos made his departure, too. It's quite con-
ceivable that they knew each other there and that the father
came to ask Sorgos some kind of favour. In which case, of
course, the son would have inherited the obligation.'

'Any evidence of direct contact?'

'No. Nor, previously, with Djugashvili, either. But, of
course, working on the waterfront, he would have plenty of
contact with the gangs, not just this one but all those working
down by the docks. He would have been just the man to go
to if you didn't know any of the gangs yourself and wanted
to be put in touch with one.'

'Did he have any other role, do you think? Other than
intermediary?'

'Nothing has come out. He has the name of being a hard
man. If you owe him a favour, you pay it. Mind you, if he
owes you one, he pays too. But they say he sticks to his own
business, which is boats. I don't see him going much outside
that. Unless, of course, it was part of returning a favour.'

'A thief, a pimp, a liar and a vagabond,' said the voice on the telephone; 'deceitful, treacherous, conniving and immoral! Nothing bad goes on in these docks and he's not there! On the fringes, perhaps, but there! And he says he's a friend of yours.'

'What's his name?' said Owen.

'Sidi.'

'Put him on.'

There was a slight pause and then a voice said uncertainly: 'Effendi?'

'I am here.'

'Effendi, this is a strange thing. I have not seen one of these before. Just *where* are you?'

'In Cairo.'

'Then you are not here?'

'You speak into that and it goes all the way to Cairo. You speak and I can hear.'

'Well, that is very remarkable. If it is true. Anyway, if this is the way you wish to talk, so let it be. Effendi, I have sad news to report.'

'Sad news?'

'The package you asked me to look out for has arrived.'

'It has? And you have found it? Well, that is good news, not sad.'

'That, unfortunately, Effendi, is not all. First, it was not I who found it. If it had been, all would have been simple. I would have told no one save you and you would have come. Unfortunately, it was Abou who found it. He told Ibrahim and Ibrahim told the men in the office, as you said. And perhaps a few other people. Or maybe it was that fool, Abou. Effendi, when I become rich, that is definitely one man I shall not employ. Even to lead the donkeys.'

'Word has got out?'

'That is right, Effendi. I said to Ibrahim, Ibrahim, this is foolish. Go to the man at the top! That is always the best course. But he would not listen to me, Effendi. He thinks I am too young. But, Effendi, intelligence is nothing to do with age, as I told him. Unfortunately, strength is, and he dealt me a blow and I thought it wisest to say nothing after that. But that meant I had to watch the box by myself—'

'You were watching the box?'

'Well, Effendi, someone had to. It was only prudent. There is a lot to the box. I suggested to Ibrahim that a watch be kept, but he said that was not necessary. So I decided I would watch by myself. Unfortunately, Effendi, the long hours—I woke up to find the box gone.'

'Gone!'

'I ran at once to the loading bay and found them putting it into a cart. And then I ran to the man in the office. But he would not listen to me, he said: "What do you know about it, foolish boy? What business is it of yours? Begone, or I shall have you beaten!" And I said: "I am not the one who will be beaten when the Mamur Zapt finds out." And then he agreed to go with me but by the time we got to the bay it was too late. The cart had gone—'

A voice cut in over Sidi's.

'Effendi, what the boy says is, alas, on this one occasion, true. It was an unfortunate misunderstanding—'

'You have let the explosives go?'

'Effendi, I—'

Chapter 11

Owen, considerably less relaxed and feeling not at all benign, sat in his office wondering where it had all gone wrong. He had been so sure of a number of things. He had been sure, for a start, that he had identified the potential troublemakers: Sorgos rousing the rabble and raising money; the Georgians down in the Der, handy when it came to action; Djugashvili, committed to the anti-Russian cause and capable, their likely leader. His agents had brought him reports of no others. They were all under constant observation and could not, positively could not, have gone to Suez and collected the explosives. There must be someone else involved.

He had been sure, too, that there was a connection between the gold-gathering and getting hold of the explosives. It all hung together. Why else had Sorgos been scratching around for gold? Why else go to the lengths of commissioning a gang to screw money out of a café? He had been so sure that by seizing the gold they had collected he would put a spoke in their wheel. Now someone had definitely put a spoke in his!

Had he been wrong all along? Was there no connection at all between the gold and the explosives? Were the explosives simply being imported for some other purpose, still, probably, nefarious but of a lesser order of criminality, at least as far as the Mamur Zapt was concerned? Tomb-robbing, say? A matter for the Parquet, not him. Perhaps he should have passed the whole thing over to Mahmoud!

But where did that leave the Grand Duke? Were Sorgos and the others completely innocent of any designs on his life? Not from what Sorgos had said. But was what Sorgos said to be trusted? Wasn't he just a crazy, cracked old man? But if so, what was he collecting gold for? Mingrelian wedding rings? And these Georgians: innocent? Well, not entirely, if Omar's identification of Djugashvili as the man who had commissioned the raid on Mustapha's café was to be trusted. But was that necessarily connected with the explosives? Maybe Djugashvili was involved in some other kind of racket.

But no, there *was* a connection between the gold and the explosives, he was sure. He was sure that was what Sorgos had been raising gold for; and he was almost sure now that that was what the raid on the café had been about, to raise money to pay for the gold.

No, that bit was right. Where he had gone wrong was in his assumption that if the plotters were prevented from paying, they would not be able to get their hands on the explosives.

Perhaps they *had* intended to pay, to buy the explosives in the normal commercial way. Perhaps they were, as Georgiades and Nikos kept saying, criminal naïfs, doing it for the first time. Perhaps that had genuinely been their plan. And then, because of his own daft action in seizing the gold, they had altered it. They had gone for the explosives directly.

That was all he could think. What it meant, though, was that the explosives were now in their hands. In their hands and there for use. Only a day ago he had been making a joke of it, mentioning the explosives only out of devilment, just to put the fear of God into Shearer. Well, he had certainly done that. Only now it had turned out not to be a joke at all but very, very real!

And he was the man who had done it.

He was the man, therefore, who must do his best to undo it. He knew what he had to do. He hated taking action like this, he was as bad as Mahmoud about preventive detention. It always seemed to him merely coercive, the antithesis of the way he normally liked to proceed, which had some sort of relation to justice.

There was no help for it, however. He got up and went into the outer office. Nikos was at his desk working. Georgiades was sitting in a corner, depressed. He looked up as Owen entered.

'Fetch me Djugashvili,' said Owen.

~~~

'What is the charge?' said Djugashvili.

'I will be handing you over to Mr. El Zaki shortly,' said Owen, 'and he will be presenting charges of inducing and inciting in connection with a raid on a café.'

He caught the quick look of relief on Djugashvili's face.

'Meanwhile, I shall be holding you under my powers with relation to security.'

'In what connection?' asked Djugashvili.

'In connection with a projected attempt on the life of Grand Duke Nicholas.'

Djugashvili shrugged.

'It's all beside the point now, isn't it?' he said bitterly.

'Why so?'

'It's all effectively come to an end, hasn't it?'

'Has it?'

'You've got the gold. We won't be able to raise another lot in time.'

Owen deliberated.

'What did you intend to do with the gold?' he said at last.

Djugashvili laughed.

'Buy explosives, of course.'

'You would still buy them?'

'I certainly would.'

'Why?' said Owen. 'When you already have them?'

Djugashvili stared at him.

'What are you talking about?'

'The explosives,' said Owen. 'They came into Suez, didn't they? And you were going to collect them. When you'd got the money. Only it had to be in gold, so it was taking a bit of time. But there the explosives were, at Suez, just waiting for you and the money.'

'Well?'

'You almost make me think,' said Owen, 'that you are not the ones who took them.'

Djugashvili looked stunned.

'Someone else?' he whispered. Then he recovered. 'Someone else!' he said. 'And they've got the explosives already?' He laughed triumphantly. 'Then it will go ahead! You cannot stop it now!'

'If not you,' said Owen, 'then who? Have you got any idea?'

'Oh, yes,' said Djugashvili. 'I've got an idea!'

'I want to know,' said Owen.

Djugashvili laughed, and was still laughing as he was taken to the cells.

⌘

The men had come at four o'clock in the afternoon when only the most alert of Cairo's citizens had risen from their post-prandial beds, and even these were still shaking the sleep from their eyes. The Nubian wrestler was possibly not one of the most alert and it was this, Selim had supposed, that had accounted for the slight delay before he arrived on the scene. In the interval Selim had fought like a lion. This was not just his own view but the view of the considerable number of spectators that gathered outside Mustapha's café in a remarkably short space of time.

According to Selim, he had been partaking of refreshment in the kitchen with Mustapha's wife when the sound of splintering wood had drawn his attention to the main room at the front. He had entered it to find two men engaged in breaking up the furniture and Mustapha prudently scuttling for the stairs. Selim had drawn his baton and laid into the two men. A lucky blow on the elbow had virtually disabled one and Selim was left free to concentrate on giving the other a taste of justice. This was proceeding very satisfactorily when three other men had burst into the room.

Things had then livened up appreciably. The expert Selim had found himself confronted by other experts. Had he been the average Cairo constable he would at this juncture sensibly have made for the back door. Selim, however, as he pointed out to Owen afterwards, was not the average Cairo constable. He was, first, bigger and, second, inclined to the robust. A mêlée with fists, feet, and furniture flying was exactly the situation in which he felt himself most at home, which was why, in fact, the inhabitants of his home village, after much experience, had pointed him strongly to a career in the Cairo constabulary and gone so far as to promise to supplement his wages if he stayed there. Faced with a challenge, and still smarting from Mustapha's taunts over what he considered his failure on the previous occasion, the last thing Selim had in mind was retreating.

Nevertheless, there *were* three of them, not to mention the two already lying groaning on the floor, and they were all, Selim soon recognized, as used as he was to this kind of thing. It was now, however, that his true colours were valiantly revealed. For he fought like a demented lion (lion, according to Selim, demented, according to the spectators). Furniture flew, chairs crashed, both on him and on his assailants, and after a hectic interval, his assailants stepped back to regroup.

Two more men appeared.

Mustapha's wife ran back into the kitchen for boiling water. Selim, still defiant, but now breathing heavily and already somewhat battered, prepared to make his last stand.

At which point the Nubian wrestler, risen, apparently, at last from his slumbers, waddled into the café.

He picked up the two men nearest him, cracked their skulls together and threw them into opposite corners of the room. He picked up another and tied his arms and legs and, possibly, his neck—or so it looked to Owen when he came upon the scene shortly afterwards—into a knot. He bounced the fourth man first off the wall, then off the ceiling and finally off himself (it was the latter that proved the *coup de grâce*); and then advanced happily on the last man, who was by this time looking for the nearest exit.

All this was very satisfactory, especially as there were two further men lying stunned outside. If only it had stopped there! Unfortunately, the Nubian wrestler, slow to rouse, was hard to quieten down again, and he was still throwing the men around when Owen arrived on the spot quite some minutes later, by which time, as Mustapha bitterly pointed out, the damage done to the café was far in excess of what it would have been if the gang had been allowed a free hand in the first place.

Owen was only able to bring things to a halt by the expedient of removing the bodies one by one as they hit the wall, so that in the end the Nubian was left with nothing else to throw. He stood for a few moments looking around him in baffled surprise and then shambled out.

⌇⌇⌇

Thus (roughly), was Selim's perception of events, recounted afterwards as he stood covered with gore and glory in the kitchen with Mustapha's wife sponging his wounds. It was not, however, entirely as he supposed. For one thing, the Nubian wrestler had not, in fact, been buried in his slumbers when the gang arrived; he had been sent on an errand by Mustapha.

'Well, I wasn't going to let that little twit go on his own, was I?' said Mustapha, defending himself. 'That tooth cost a lot of money.'

The tooth was the one he had lost in the initial fracas at the café. Mustapha had made up his mind that the time had come to restore it to its rightful position and had sent Mekhmet with it to see the dentist with instructions to prepare it for reinsertion.

'No sense in getting a new one, is there? Gold is gold.'

In view of the tooth's value, he had decided to provide Mekhmet with an escort, a factor which, as Selim, aggrieved, observed, had weakened the café's defences at a crucial point and contributed in no small measure to the damage the café had sustained. Mustapha's wife added in support that Mustapha had only himself to blame, for he had sent the two men out in the hottest part of the day when any reasonable man knew they could not be expected to hurry.

Hurried they had not, for the wrestler found it necessary to stop at various points to refresh himself with cheap Sudanese *marissa* beer, with the result that as they were approaching home on their return journey he had been obliged to go up a side street to relieve his bladder. It had thus been Mekhmet alone who had entered the street just as the storyteller was pointing out the café to the gang. He had run back at once to fetch the wrestler but by then precious time had been lost.

'Just a moment,' said Owen. 'Pointing out the café?'

Nonsense, said the storyteller. He had just been passing the time of day. Alternatively, supposing that they were in search of somewhere they could sit down and have a cup of coffee, he had merely been responding politely to their enquiries. Anyway, that little twit had got it wrong.

'Would you like to talk to me here?' asked Owen. 'Or shall I send you with Selim to the Bab-el-Khalk and talk to you there?'

After one glance at Selim, the storyteller decided that he would prefer to talk to Owen here, so Owen took him to an upstairs room—the room in which Mustapha had been lying when he had first seen him, posted Selim on the stairs to keep out the curious, and told Mustapha to get on with clearing up the café.

Then he turned to the storyteller.

'So, my friend,' he said, 'how does it work?'

The storyteller looked around him desperately, swallowed and then decided there was nothing else for it.

'It works,' he said, 'in all sorts of ways. Sometimes they come to us, sometimes we go to them. Usually, they come to us. "Know any good places?" they say. Well, of course, we know all the cafés and, sitting out the front as we do, we see who goes in and have a pretty good idea of how much money the café is taking. We might say: "That one's been doing well lately, it's come on a bit." Or we might say: "I wouldn't try that one, it's not worth your while." Or sometimes,' said the storyteller, waxing, '"Don't go there, it's just a poor old woman on her own, lame and suffering, plagued with boils—"'

'I weep,' said Owen.

The storyteller looked hurt.

'I'm just telling you the way it is,' he said. 'I wouldn't want you to think we are hard of heart or unjust. We spare the poor and charge the rich. We see some fat man growing fatter, and we say: "Pick on him! He can stand it." If it wasn't for us,' said the storyteller virtuously, 'they might pick on the wrong people.'

'All you are doing is making the world a juster place?'

'Exactly!' agreed the storyteller, pleased.

'For a suitable fee, no doubt?'

'Not much of one. Enough to buy a crust of bread, perhaps. Or a bowl of *durra* when things go hard and we can't get a job. Times are often hard,' said the storyteller sadly, 'for storytellers.'

'I weep again. But tell me; you say "we". Do all storytellers, then, do as you do?'

'No, no, no. Only those of us who are—'

The storyteller stopped.

'Organized?'

'Well—'

'There is an organization, then, for storytellers?'

'Only for some storytellers,' said the man reluctantly.

'And who are they?'

The storyteller swallowed.

'If I went to a storyteller who was *not* organized,' prompted Owen gently, 'no doubt he would tell me who *were* organized. So why don't you tell me?'

'We're trying to break in,' said the storyteller reluctantly.

'Ah!' said Owen. 'Now I think I begin to understand. You are the storytellers who are telling the new stories?'

'That's right.'

'You tell neither the stories of Abu Zeyd nor the stories of the Sultan Baybars?'

'That is correct.'

'I have heard some of your stories,' said Owen, 'and like them.'

'You do?' said the storyteller, pleased. 'Well, they are rather good. Take, for instance, the story of—'

'Well, not just now, perhaps. We are talking of other matters. The stories you tell: where do they come from?'

'They are old stories. They are the ones we heard as children, the ones that were on our mother's lips.'

'You are remembering them, then?'

'Well, it's not always easy to remember them when you are old. You remember pieces of them, fragments.'

'So what do you do?'

'Well—'

'You go to someone, perhaps, who has a store of these old stories?'

'Well, yes. It's not quite as simple as that, though. We have a piece of an old story and we give it in, and it may be that another man has a different piece, so that the two pieces can be put together and perhaps fitted into a third—'

'And then you share the complete story?'

'Yes.'

'Which is written out for you?'

'Well, you can get a copy, and I'm not saying that some storytellers don't do that. But I don't like that myself. It's not the proper way. No, you hear the story, you hear it once or twice, and then you've more or less got it. You take it away and, well, you do things with it, you sort of make it your own.'

'A storyteller of distinction,' said Owen, 'always tells his own story.'

'Absolutely right! That's what I always say. And that's why there ought to be different prices for different storytellers. The trouble is,' said the storyteller, eloquent on this particular subject at least, 'that there are too many people in the market right now. It brings the prices down. Oh, they're not bad, some of them, but the worst ones drag the prices down. People are prepared to settle for any old sort of rubbish these days.'

'And then, of course,' said Owen, 'the old storytellers, the Abu Zeyd ones and the Sultan Baybars ones, are so established! It must be hard to break in.'

'Oh it is! That's why—'

He stopped.

'That's why you have to join together?'

'Well, yes.'

'It is like a sort of club, isn't it? By joining together you can help each other.'

'Yes.'

'Tell me, when you say to a gang: "Such and such a place would be a good one to try," do they pay you directly or does the money go to the club?'

'It goes to the club.'

'And then the club pays you?'

'Yes. Not all the money. Some is put aside for us to draw on when we are old or sick.'

'You think that? You think that it will really be there?'

'Some was given to Faroukh when he was sick.'

'Ah! So it is really there. At the moment. Tell me who is the master of the club?'

The storyteller was silent.

'He who keeps the store of stories?'

'Well—'

'I marvel,' said Owen. 'I had always thought those who lived by story were upright men.'

'It may have been so,' said the storyteller, 'in the time of Sultan Baybars.'

⟨∞⟩

The bookshop was in a small street off the Clot Bey. The street was near the Coptic church and some of the other shops dealt in relics. Owen looked to see and, yes, one or two stocked ikons. The bookshop contained some Coptic books, displayed prominently at the front in an effort to tap the Coptic custom, but since the books were chiefly theological and in Old Coptic, Owen thought it unlikely that sales were prolific. Inside the shop, the books were lined on shelves, as in a European bookshop. There was a musty smell in the air and the books, too, were old and musty: French and Arabic equivalents of the Coptic works seen from outside. European in style the shop might be; nevertheless, it came as something of a shock to see that the assistant was a woman. Despite the veil, Owen recognized Katarina.

He went inside and began to look along the shelves.

Katarina came up to him.

'Why can't you leave us alone?' she hissed.

'I need your help.'

'I've told you—'

'They've got hold of explosives. I thought they would be safe in Suez docks until they were paid for. That's why I took the gold. I hoped I could stop it all without it coming to anything. But the explosives have slipped through. Someone's got hold of them. I must find out who that someone is.'

'Why ask me?'

'You know who Sorgos meets.'

'I know you have seized Djugashvili.'

'It's someone else.'

'Why do you keep coming to me? I will not help you. I have told you, I am with my grandfather.'

'In everything?'

'Yes!'

'In explosives?'

'Yes!'

'Please help me.'

Katarina looked around wildly. A man came forward out of the darkness at the back of the shop.

'Can I help, my dear?'

'The Mamur Zapt!' said Katarina. 'My father!' she said to Owen.

'Your father!'

'The Mamur Zapt!'

'I thought you were in Paris!' said Owen.

The man recovered and came forward with outstretched hand.

'I was. I have only just returned. Two days ago.'

He shook hands with Owen.

'And not a moment before time,' he said, 'if what I hear is true.'

'I wrote to him,' said Katarina.

'I came at once. How could I not? My father—what can I say? He is an old man and, not to put too fine a point upon it, no longer responsible for his actions.'

'He has always seemed to me exceptionally alert.'

'That is kind of you. But he has, I know, caused you considerable alarm. At a time when, I imagine, you would have preferred to have been preoccupied by more serious matters.'

'You think the alarm was unnecessary?'

'Well …' Katarina's father spread his hands. 'Passions are running high over the Grand Duke, I know, and I daresay my father's passions have been running higher than most, but I feel you may have been mistaking rhetoric for action—'

'I know what the gold was for,' said Owen.

Katarina's father went still.

Then he sighed.

'Well,' he said, 'why deny it? Since you know so much? But, Captain Owen, can I plead with you to make allowances? He is a very old man. I thought he could defy time forever but, coming back, after an absence, I see...Captain Owen, will you allow me to take the blame for whatever my father has done? I am the man responsible. I should not have left him. If I had been here, none of this would have occurred.'

'He would have felt differently?'

Katarina's father made a gesture of hopelessness.

'He would have felt exactly the same. But I would have restrained him. Captain Owen, is it too late? I promise that I will see he is no trouble to you. He will not leave the house until the Grand Duke's visit is over. I promise you that. That is the least I can do and I assure you that it will be done.'

'That may be for the best. My concern, I should say, is less about him than about others.'

'Concentrate on them, Captain Owen, and leave me to take care of my father. He will be no further trouble to you, I assure you. Let me be his guarantor.'

'Very well.'

'Thank you. And thank you for your sympathy and understanding. My father, as I am sure you know, speaks very warmly of you.'

'Even now?'

Katarina's father smiled.

'Less warmly, perhaps.' He glanced at the book Owen was holding in his hand. 'Can I help you?'

He took the book.

'The *Mabinogion*? Oh, of course, I was forgetting: my father told me you were Welsh.'

'I am afraid the impression your father has of Wales may not be altogether accurate.'

'No. Katarina has been telling me!' He laughed. 'He is right, though; the parallels are there. What makes a people? Language, as my father believes? Language is certainly significant but it is not all there is to Wales. Land? Important, too, but what about the Jews? Culture? I quite favour that myself, but'—he looked at the book again—'culture can sometimes be a thing of the past. Oh, I know you will point to the Eisteddfod, you will say that things are still being written in Welsh, but—'

'You make culture too narrow a thing.'

'I tie it to language. That, perhaps, is my mistake. But even so, Captain Owen, I have a problem with Wales. The English came and took away the politics. What they left was the culture. But can there be culture without politics? I ask that because that in a way is the debate you are having with my father.'

He smiled.

'I can say that because I am having the debate, too. I am for culture as opposed to politics. All the same, I cannot quite escape my father's question. General question, that is.'

'Are the Welsh a nation?'

'You make it particular again. But, yes, that is the question. However, let us not go to war over it. There have been too many wars over such things already.'

Chapter 12

The first part of the Grand Duke's visit had passed off without incident. He had arrived at Alexandria, transferred to the Khedivial Yacht and sailed to Suez; entrained to Cairo, spent two happy days, everyone was sure, with the Khedive in the Abdin Palace, and then embarked in a dahabeeyah, especially done up for the occasion at expense which made the Financial Comptroller tear his hair, for Luxor. All without being assailed.

So far, thought Owen, so good. It was the next bit, though, after his return to Cairo, that would be crucial. The time when he would be most exposed would be during the procession and it was then, if anywhere, thought Owen, that the attack would come. He had delegated responsibility, a shrewd political move, no doubt, but one that left him slightly uncomfortable. Passing the formal buck was all very well, but at the end of the day there was still the question of real responsibility and Owen had a disagreeable feeling that it was his.

He had salved his conscience by doing all he could. His agents were everywhere in force. If there had been any whisper of a threat it would have been picked up by them. In the bazaars, however, which Owen regarded as the only accurate source of information in Cairo, there was no whisper. The initial barrage of protests made by ex-citizens of countries he had never heard of had died away. The only real follow-up his spies had detected had been that of Sorgos and his adherents in the Der of Babylon.

There, too, he had done what he could. Sorgos, if Katarina's father was to be believed, and, certainly, so far he had kept his word, was safely confined to his house. Djugashvili was under lock and key. Other Georgians, most notably the restorers, were under constant observation. If it had not been for the explosives he would have felt he had things more or less under control.

But they were out there somewhere. And there, too, somewhere, was the other player in this game, the man or men whom Djugashvili knew but who somehow operated independently of him and the other people in the Der. Where were the explosives now, he wondered? In the Der, very probably. He had considered a search but Nikos had warned him in unusually strong terms against any such thing. It would provoke a riot, he said. The Copts in the Der, he said— and, after all, they were his own kind—discriminated imperfectly between one invader and another. Intrusion was a thing they would resist, whether it was by Saladdin, the Mamelukes, the Turks or the British. Keep out, he had advised. And Georgiades had reinforced this by pointing to the extreme difficulty of finding anything concealed in so labyrinthine a place. Tunnels, caves, pits, passages, he said, you'd need an army to get anywhere.

So Owen had ruled out a search. He was still, however, unhappy and had even gone to the lengths of tracing on foot the route the procession was going to take, noting carefully points at which explosives might be placed. On the day itself he would have men placed in as many of these points as he could. Cairo was Cairo, however, and although the procession would keep to the wider streets as far as it could, inevitably there were places where the old houses crowded in and the heavy, box-like *meshrebiya* windows overhung the route, which made it a nightmare to guard against bomb-throwing.

Again, he did what he could. Still, at the end, though, the doubt remained. Something still nagged.

He realized at last what it was. The question he had asked himself before still remained unanswered. Why had they chosen explosives in the first place? A bullet would have been much easier and was, if his impression of the life Sorgos and his friends had led in the Caucasus was at all accurate, a much more natural thing for them to use. Why go to all this trouble?

It must, surely, be something to do with the way in which they planned to end their adversary: the Grand Duke's Grand Finale.

Why explosives?

৩৩৩৩

At the end of the corridor, sounds of a scuffle. Voices saying, 'No, you don't!' More scuffle. The door of the Orderly Room banging shut. Period of silence.

Broken by the sound of something hitting the shutters of his window. A bird?

Again! What the hell was this? Couldn't be a bird, not twice, not unless it was hell bent on suicide. Again! Bloody hell, someone was throwing things at his window!

He leaped up and threw open the shutters. There, in the yard below, was a small figure he dimly recognized.

'Effendi! Effendi! You remember me? Sidi!'

Sidi?

'From the docks! You remember?'

Orderlies came tearing round the corner.

'Hold on! Wait a minute! Bring him to me!'

Voices again in the corridor.

'It's bloody amputation for you! We practise Sharia law here!'

A dishevelled Sidi appeared in the doorway.

'Effendi, they would not let me speak to you!'

'How the hell did you get here?'

'The train, Effendi. I sat between the wheels.'

'All the way? Christ!'

'It was important, Effendi. My honour had been besmirched. Not that it was my fault, it was those dolts in the office. Worse than dolts: knaves!'

'You came all the way here to see me?'

'What else could I do, Effendi? I had to speak with you and it would not have been wise to ask the man to let me use that thing we used before. Besides, Effendi, with that thing words can be passed, but can piastres be passed? Not,' said Sidi virtuously, 'that we are talking of piastres. Not when my honour is concerned!'

'How is your honour concerned?'

'I had said I would watch over the box. True, it was only to myself that I had said it but I knew you would be expecting good things of me. Was it accident, I asked myself, that you had spoken to me? Sought my help in the first place? Heard my words? Treated me as a man with men and said I would receive the reward if I earned it? You had given me your trust, Effendi, and how had I rewarded it? By falling asleep at the crucial moment. And so the box was taken. You did not upbraid me, Effendi, but I upbraided myself.'

'The fault was not yours.'

'No, it was not. For whereas my fault was that of accident, theirs was the fault of design.'

'How could that be?'

'Because, Effendi, it was not through mischance that the box was released. A man came before and spoke to those in the office. And afterwards Abdulla Arbat went home and boasted of it, saying: "I have done a good deed this day and am the richer for it."'

'How do you know this?'

'Because Sayid Sarmani saw the man come and Ahmet Arja heard the words.'

'Who is Sayid?'

'A friend, Effendi, as is Ahmet. Sayid was sitting in the road when the man came and he saw him again when the box was taken. And Ahmet's sister lives next door to Abdulla

Arbat and he was with her when Abdulla came home. They were out in the yard and they heard Abdulla come and speak to his wife and say: "Bring me beer, for fortune has smiled on me." And then he said that he had done a good deed and was the richer for it.'

'So the sister heard too?'

'Yes, though her word cannot be relied on as can that of a man.'

'And what about the words of your two friends? Can they be relied on?'

'Sayid speaks truthfully, Effendi, although, between us, he is never going to soar to the heights of donkey man. He is a little slow, Effendi, though willing. Ahmet, on the other hand, is no fool. He notices what he sees. When I am rich, Effendi, I might even consider employing Ahmet.'

'And does he speak the truth?'

'When he is among friends, Effendi.'

'I will, I think, speak with this man, Abdulla.'

'Do so, Effendi. You will find him a big bladder of wind. But he will tell you, I think, that a certain man came to him and gave him money that he might take the box away without the gate-man asking him questions.'

'The gate-man, too, then, could have a story to tell?'

'He will tell it, Effendi, only if he knows that it is useless to deny it.'

'I will speak to Abdulla first, then. And thank you, Sidi, for all you have told me.'

'Effendi, I know I do not merit the entire reward—'

'But you merit some of it. And shall have it.'

'I had hopes, Effendi, of buying a donkey.'

'Hope, even of two,' said Owen.

৬৩৩৩৯

Improper. The Orderly Room was shocked.

'A woman,' said Nikos, disapprovingly. 'Alone,' he added with emphasis.

Everyone knew that a woman should not speak for herself. If she had business to transact, it should be done through her nearest male relative; if there were no male relatives, then through a friend or a senior figure in the community. Where would we be if women took it upon themselves to urge their own causes? Things would fall apart and the centre would not hold.

On the other hand, this lady was plainly not for turning, at least, not turning away. After their experience with Sidi, the Orderly Room had lost a little confidence, and the issue was put to Nikos. Nikos was not at his best in anything to do with women. He was not especially against them, he was not particularly for them. He was puzzled, in fact, why they had been made. One thing was clear, however; they had been made second, and this was good enough excuse for Nikos not having got round to them yet. In office management, prioritization was all.

He would, therefore, have postponed the matter, and, indeed, gone on postponing it until the woman went away. She showed obstinate signs, however, of staying. Worse, she said that she was acquainted with the Mamur Zapt, which, if true, meant that the Mamur Zapt was acquainted with her. If, now, he denied her access, who knows through what disreputable route communication might be made? Better to have it here, where Nikos could keep a controlling eye on things.

'A woman,' said Nikos unwillingly. 'Alone,' he added, in a voice which indicated both the gravity of the situation and disapproval.

'Show her in,' said Owen, preoccupied with other things and therefore unaware of the heavy currents swirling about the office.

In came the woman, shapeless black from head to foot, heavily veiled with the double veil, the one that went up and the one that came down, covering head, shoulders and front almost down to the waist. Something might still be detected;

height, for instance. The woman was taller than the usual Egyptian; in fact—?

'Leave us.'

Katarina threw back the top over-veil.

'How about the other one?'

Above the other veil, however, Katarina's eyes did not respond.

He handed her to a chair, which she sank down on almost with relief.

'What's the trouble?' he asked.

She didn't reply at once. She just sat there looking at him, as if she was weighing him up.

'Coffee?'

She shook her head.

He went across to the pitcher of water cooling in the window and passed her a glass. She took it but did not drink. She still seemed to be studying him.

He pulled up a chair opposite her, sat down and waited.

'You were right,' she said suddenly. 'There are explosives.'

'The ones that came in through Suez?'

She nodded.

'They have been brought to Cairo.'

'And are in the Der?'

'Yes,' she said, 'they are in the Der.'

'Do you know where?'

'Yes,' she said, 'I know where.'

'Can you show me?'

She did not reply at once. Owen did not press.

'Will it be as you say?' she suddenly burst out. 'That they will kill a lot of people?'

'It depends how they are used,' he said. 'But, yes, they could kill a lot of people.'

He waited, and then, as she did not speak, he said, 'Have you any idea how they are going to be used?'

She shook her head.

'I just know they are there.'

'And will be used.'

She nodded slowly.

'Unless you tell me.'

He could see she was hesitating.

'I would tell you,' she said, 'if only I could be sure—'

'What do you want to be sure about?'

'There are people,' she said. 'I want to give you the explosives; but I don't want to give you the people.'

'The explosives are what matter,' said Owen. 'No explosives, no killing. Although even then we could not be sure. It would be better if I knew the people.'

She shook her head.

'It has to be a deal,' she said. 'I tell you about the explosives; you don't ask me about the people.'

'Very well, I accept that.'

'Also,' she stipulated, 'you don't use the knowledge to trap the people.'

'It is hard to separate knowledge out. What if I already have knowledge? How can I set that aside?'

'What I meant,' she said, 'was that you must not set a trap for them. You must not lie in wait for them.'

'It might be better if I did.'

She shook her head firmly.

'No,' she said. 'You must promise me that. Otherwise I shall tell you nothing.'

'What if I take them by other means?'

He was afraid she was going to stipulate an immunity but she did not.

'If you find out in other ways,' she said in a low voice, 'let it be so. But you must not take them through any action of mine.'

'I give you my promise.'

She put her hand up to her face, unclipped the veil and took a drink of water. Then she replaced the veil and stood up.

'Let us go then,' she said.

Once again Owen found himself in the Fustat, and once again he lost himself in the narrow, overhung streets and had to find his way to the ferry for orientation. He realized suddenly that in this part of the Fustat that was what you did. Everyone thought instinctively in terms of the river. The smell of the river lingered in the dark streets, the tall masts of the gyassas tied to the bank hung over the low houses. The little alleyways all led down to the river.

The river was the centre of people's lives. It provided work for the men, whether as boatmen working the little boats that went to and fro across the river with vegetables or fish, or the bigger gyassas that went up and down the Nile carrying grain, or as porters unloading the grain in its gaily patterned biscuit-coloured sacks, or as boat builders working with little bits of wood not much bigger than bricks out of which most Nile boats were built. There were rope yards and tarring pits, porters' cafés such as the one in which the gang had had its headquarters, lettuce carts waiting for the vegetables to be unloaded, sentry boxes protecting men from the sun as they sold the water from the public taps—and, of course, the low dancing booths with their low ladies.

It had never quite come home to him before how different this part of Cairo was, different from the modern city which was hardly orientated to the river at all, different, too, from the world of the Ders which was only a few hundred yards away. The difference could be seen in the attitudes to thoroughfares. For the dock people, the Nile was the great thoroughfare along which all traffic flowed. In the Ders there were no thoroughfares, there were hardly any streets. You passed from building to building by going through underground passages, from vault to vault. There was nothing by which to orientate yourself. You had to know the way.

Once she was in the Der, Katarina did. More surely than Georgiades, she picked her way through the cloisters and tunnels until they came out into the sunlight and saw up above them the magnificent curtain wall of the old Roman fortress and the great arch of the old Roman gate. He knew now where he was; and was not so very surprised to find himself climbing once more the handsome staircase which swept up to the Hanging Church, the Mo'allaka.

Once more he saw the antique swinging lamps with their tiny flames, the golden ikons, the slender outlines of the delicate marble pulpit standing out against the overpowering richness of the dark screen, the low Moresco arches outlined with ivory which led into the sanctuary.

He looked across the church to the corner where the restorers had been working, but this time there was no subdued lamp, nothing moved in the darkness.

Katarina led him across the church and behind the screen. There was space to walk and giving off the space were various little cabinets or chapels. One had an image of the Virgin, soft and delicate, painted by Roman hands before dour Byzantine ideas crushed human outlines out of holy faces. Another had a strange painted cabinet with a lamp swaying in front of it, and wooden drums like shells for modern field guns which contained holy relics. Ostrich eggs hung from the roof.

To the left of the sanctuary was a low arch, so low that Katarina had to stoop deeply to go through it and Owen had to go down almost on to his knees. There was no light and for a moment or two he could not tell where he was. But then he saw the top of a very large tank and realized that he was in the baptismal room. Copts baptized by immersion.

He advanced cautiously to the tank and looked down, expecting to see water. There was, however, only a dry, cold musty smell. The tank had not been used for many years.

On one side of the tank, going down into it, there were wooden *meshrebiya* steps, slippery smooth to the touch. Katarina directed his hand down beneath them. He groped uncertainly but found nothing.

Katarina put her own hand down, gave a little surprised gasp and then clambered down into the tank. He could feel her scrabbling at the bottom.

Then she stood up.

'They've gone,' she said.

༺ singular decoration ༻

In the church a priest was lighting candles.

'The restorers!' said Owen. 'Where are they?'

The priest looked up, surprised.

'Aren't they here? They were here. The workshops, perhaps?'

Owen ran down the stairs. In the courtyard a donkey was contentedly cropping the foliage that pushed through the trellis. The workshop was empty.

Back in the courtyard he found the donkey's owner washing his face in the fountain.

'Peace be with you!' he said.

'And with you, peace!'

'I am looking for two men. They work in the church here.'

'Do they wear boots?'

'Yes.'

The donkey's owner nodded.

'I know them.'

'They are neither Arab nor Copt.'

'They wear boots,' said the man, picking out the—for him—salient thing.

'That is so. And I look for them.'

'You are fortunate, then, for I have seen them.'

'This morning?'

'But shortly. As I was coming in at the gate.'

'Were they carrying anything?'

'Not they, but their donkey. Two heavy bags that made the donkey groan.'

'They would go slowly, then.'

'Slower still, were it not for the donkey.'

The gate was still the tremendous gate of the Roman builders. Its columns dwarfed the steady stream of passers-through below and were large enough to admit even heavy stone carts, although what happened to them once they had entered, and how they managed with the low arches and tunnels, Owen could not think. There was the usual crowd of beggars at the gate and to them Owen made application.

Two men with a donkey? Alas, there were many men with donkeys, too many to recall, Effendi. With boots? Ah, that was a different matter. Two men, neither Copt nor Arab, had passed through the gate scarcely more than an hour since.

The direction? As, in the Fustat, you would expect. The Effendi was not in the Der now. All roads in the Fustat led not to Babylon but to the river.

And there was the river ahead of him, glinting in the sunlight, with a felucca stooping and skimming—and then it disappeared, and as always near the docks, he lost his way in the medieval alleys as the houses crowded together overhead and he lost sight even of the masts rising up along the river bank. He had to ask the way, yet again, to the ferry.

Two men, neither Arab nor Copt, in boots and with a donkey? There was the usual crowd of onlookers at the ferry, but this time he drew a blank.

Well, they had not gone over the ferry, then. He walked along the waterfront, repeating his question.

And then he saw two men ahead of him whom he recognized. They were not the Georgians but his own men, the men who had been keeping them under observation. They were gazing stupidly out across the water.

'Effendi, they got on to a boat! And another with them!'
'Another?' said Owen.

Boats, on the river, were as distinguishable as donkeys in a village. Other men had seen the boat put out and some of them were knowledgeable waterfront men. They were able to identify the boat immediately.

'It belongs to Hussein al-Fadal, Effendi,' they said.

'Hussein al-Fadal? Ah, I have heard of him.'

'Who has not heard of him, Effendi? In this part of the Fustat, anyway.'

'Where is the boat bound for?'

'It is one of his ordinary boats. They go up to Assuan.'

Which seemed at first not to be particularly helpful. Why would the Georgians want to take explosives up to Assuan? Was it, perhaps, after all, that they merely intended to take them further, to sell them, perhaps, to potential insurgents in the Sudan? If so, that would be reprehensible, certainly, and must be stopped; but it was nothing to do with the Grand Duke.

Unless…

༄

In other circumstances Owen would have relished the journey. Views differed about the best way to travel on the Nile; some favoured Mr. Cook's new steamers, which were certainly very comfortable, others the traditional dahabeeyah, which was how most tourists had made the journey upriver until comparatively recently. For Owen, though, there was nothing like a felucca. It was a much smaller craft than most of those on the river, taking only three or four men, and with its low sides and its tall mast—most of the sailing boats on the Nile had tall masts to lift their sails above the palm trees which lined the river in some places—it seemed to plane over the water.

Speed was what decided it. The Georgians were travelling in a gyassa, a heavy grain boat but one which carried a lot of sail and, going before the wind, could travel with surprising speed. Going by steamer was out of the question since they were tied to a tourist timetable. In the end, Owen had decided to go by train for the first part of the journey, as far as Minia, and then switch to felucca.

The train, too, had its timetable but it was faster than going by boat and when they went down to the port they found that the gyassa had not yet arrived.

Towards evening it crept in and tied up to the landing stage. No one disembarked. Owen had not really expected them to. The gyassa was on its outward journey and would pick up the cargo somewhere beyond Assuan. It was, of course, possible that the Georgians might choose this as the place but somehow he did not expect them to. The Grand Duke's boat was still some way upriver.

In the morning the gyassa pulled out and set sail; and this time Owen set sail with it.

With him in the felucca were Georgiades and Selim, apart from the crew. That was all the felucca could take. Owen had other men but he had sent them on to Assyut by train.

It was at Assyut that he thought that the attack might take place for it was there that Duke Nicholas's dahabeeyah would tie up for the night preparatory to his visit the following day to the monuments at Beni Hassan and the cat cemetery at Speos Artemides. The stop at Assyut the Georgians might know about, since the Grand Duke's itinerary would be common talk on the river, and they might be able to guess at the excursions on the following day, although they would not be sure of them. The Duke might have had enough of visits by then.

For the moment Owen was content to keep the gyassa in view as they skimmed gently up the river. The wind, from the north as usual, had died down and the gyassa laboured. The lighter felucca soon overtook it but Owen would not let it get too far ahead.

❦

With the wind light and the flow of the river against them strong, it took two days for the gyassa to get to Assyut. They passed the night tied up to the bank with only the mosquitoes to keep them company, although Owen enjoyed the pelicans next morning. Georgiades did not. He was a city man and such excursions as this only served to confirm his prejudice. Selim, a country boy, breathed in the air as if he had forgotten what it was.

'These peasants!' he said scornfully, however, as they passed some fellahin working in the fields. 'Not bad!' he said appreciatively though as they came upon some women walking down to the river with large jars balanced on their heads, an opportunity for them to display and Selim to evaluate.

As they approached Assyut he saw ahead of him the outlines of the new barrage. The ends springing out from the banks had been joined the previous year and the barrage was just about operational though there was still building on it to be completed. Part of the idea of the Grand Duke's visit (or the Khedive's idea of the Grand Duke's visit) was to see the works of modern Egypt and this was one of the most remarkable. The Khedive had considered asking the Grand Duke to officially open it, until it was pointed out that he himself was going to open it later on in the year. Besides, if Duke Nicholas opened it, the Khedive himself would have to be present and that meant travelling south at the hottest time of the year. The Khedive decided to postpone the pleasure.

Since the Grand Duke would be passing, however, *he* could have the pleasure at least of inspecting the barrage. His dahabeeyah had arrived the previous evening and there it was, tied up at the entrance to the vast new lock which the steamers would use. His Royal Highness had spent the day seeing over the works and, no doubt, would shortly be returning to his dahabeeyah to collapse in comfort.

The gyassa had arrived in the afternoon when all work, indeed, life, was at a standstill and there were few people about to see the three men, in boots and carrying two heavy bags, walk down the gangway and on to the bank. From there they made their way into the town and entered a low house near the mile-long bazaar. They did not emerge from it until well after the sun had set in glorious red and gold upon the river and the Duke was already on his third ice-cooled vodka.

There was some delay while a donkey was obtained but once it was loaded they set off through the dark streets. If there was anything unusual about the scene it was only that men were working.

When they came to the entrance of the lock they sat down and waited. Some twenty yards from the shore the Grand Duke's great dahabeeyah turned slowly in the flow of the river, reached the limit of its mooring ropes and then turned back again. There were lights on the vessel and occasionally through the windows one caught the flash of tureens and the scurrying white of suffragis—the Duke had gone native to the extent that while on board he had allowed himself to be served by local Egyptians. Fairly local, that was, for crew, suffragis and servants belonged, like the boat itself, to a Levantine millionaire who had lent it to the Khedive for the occasion.

The men on the bank sat on in silence until gradually the activity on the dahabeeyah subsided and one by one the lights went out.

Then they stirred.

Two of them went off along the river bank and a little later returned in a small boat, inexpertly but quietly paddled, nudging its way along the river's edge. The third man, meanwhile, had been bent over the bags.

One of the men got out of the boat and came up the bank. He and the man left on shore picked up one of the bags and began to carry it down to the water.

And then dark figures were all around them.

Chapter 13

'Before you depart,' said Owen, 'there are one or two things I would like to know. Small things first: how did you know the explosives had arrived in the docks?'

'The man in the office was looking out for them,' said Katarina's father.

'Abdulla Arbat? What was he looking out for?'

'A consignment from Aleppo marked Baking Powder. He had the names, fictitious, of course, of consigner and consignee.'

'You were paying him, naturally?'

'Naturally.'

'And then you collected them yourself. Unwise, surely?'

'Unwise,' Katarina's father agreed. 'But then, time was short and there were so few people I could trust. And I was in Suez myself, having just disembarked.'

'It gave us a positive identification.'

'The boy?' Katarina's father looked glum. 'The problem was that time was so short! I would have had to get people from Cairo and I knew that you were having them watched. Besides, by that time I felt that I had better do it myself. So many things had gone wrong. Mishandled! I'm not blaming my father, but there were so many things he didn't know. Gold, for instance! My God, when I heard—! And Djugashvili was not much better. They'd never done anything criminal in their lives before.'

'Whereas you—?'

Katarina's father laughed.

'The trouble was that I was in Paris. It all blew up very suddenly, you see: the Grand Duke's visit, the idea that this might give us a chance to strike back—'

'Whose was the idea?'

Katarina's father looked at him.

'I shan't tell you,' he said. 'At first I thought, well, a good idea but I'm too far away and there isn't time to organize anything. But then when I heard there was support—'

'Not as much support as you supposed.'

'No,' Katarina's father agreed, 'not as much as I supposed.'

'Your father's enthusiasm ran away with him.'

'Perhaps. His letters at first were optimistic and confident. Good young men, he said, men of action. Well, we know, don't we,' said Katarina's father, looking at Owen, 'that men of action are a lot rarer than men of words. Intelligent action, at any rate. And so it proved.' He shook his head. 'At first I thought I could stay out of it, that they would manage without me. I thought it might even be better if I stayed in Paris, doing things from afar. I knew by that time that you were interested in my father. I thought it would be better for me to stay behind the scenes.'

'And so it would have been.'

Katarina's father spread his hands.

'But then things began to go wrong. They had problems finding money for the explosives—'

'You had money,' said Owen. 'Why didn't you pay?'

'I would have done. But at that time I thought it wasn't a problem. My father assured me—'

'Ever optimistic!' said Owen.

'Yes, ever optimistic. Besides'—he broke off and gave Owen a quick look—'you may not believe this, but I thought of the money as not being mine but the storytellers'. What I was in it for was for the stories, not for the money. The money I meant to be theirs. It was a genuine Benefit Society—'

'Criminal,' said Owen.

'Well, yes, criminal. But—'

'Tell me about the explosives. Why did you hit on them in the first place?'

'Why not a bullet, you mean?' Katarina's father sighed. 'Their idea, not mine. They wanted the Duke to go out with as big a bang as possible. The bigger the bang, they thought, the greater the attention that would be paid—to the Mingrelians, to what Russia had been doing in the Caucasus. They seemed so pleased with the idea that I did not intervene. Besides, I thought there was more chance of them succeeding with a bomb. You have to get it just right with a bullet, and already I was beginning to have doubts—'

'One thing that puzzles me,' said Owen: 'Djugashvili. I pulled him in, as you know, and when I spoke to him he did not seem to know that you had already got hold of the explosives.'

'He didn't know. When I landed at Suez I found a message from my father awaiting me. He was in despair. You had just seized the gold and he thought this was the end. Well, I was in Suez and I knew Abdulla Arbat of old, so I decided to act. No one knew about it till later.'

Owen nodded.

Katarina's father hesitated.

'May I ask when you knew?'

'About you?'

'Yes.'

'I was looking for someone else. Near Sorgos. I ruled you out, first because you were abroad and then because, well, I got the impression from your father that you were bookish—'

'Ineffectual?'

'Well, yes.'

Katarina's father smiled.

'He still thinks I'm ineffectual.'

'And not greatly interested in the kinds of battles he wants to fight.'

'Well, in a way he's right. I wasn't altogether misleading you when I said in the shop the other day that the battles I wanted to fight were cultural ones.'

'Nevertheless, you came down on his side in the end.'

'On the side of political action?'

'Violence.'

'Yes. I'm still not happy about it.'

'Well, you'll have plenty of opportunity to think it over, won't you?'

Katarina's father shrugged.

'Actually,' said Owen, 'you did not mislead me. Rather the reverse. You see, I already knew about you and the story-tellers. If I had had any notion that you were merely bookish, in your father's sense, that had already been dispelled. I had been looking for a manager, someone who was giving the whole thing direction. At first I thought it might be Djugashvili but he always seemed too limited, a man of the Der. When I met you and realized that you were here, back in Cairo, I began to wonder. And when you went to such pains to direct attention away from yourself, even at the expense of your father, I began to suspect.'

'I should have stayed behind the scenes.'

'Or out of it.'

'What will you do with my father?'

'Release him.'

'And Katarina?'

'Leave her alone.'

'Not too alone, I hope,' said Katarina's father politely. Sorgos's son and Mingrelian to the last.

~

The procession wheeled left at the Bab-el-Louk. Ahead of him Owen could see the wide open space of Abdin Square.

Once there he could afford to relax. The square was lined with soldiers and anyway, the procession, crossing straight across the middle, would be sufficiently far from the crowd for only the steadiest shot to succeed, and in Cairo assassins' hands were often fervent but seldom steady. At the other end of the square was Abdin Palace and once there, behind its iron railings, the Khedive and the Grand Duke would be safe.

It was, actually, the Khedive that Owen was worried about more. For the most part he stayed prudently out of sight of his people, seldom appearing in public, and the opportunity to take a pot shot at him might prove irresistible. The same thought had occurred to the Khedive himself of the previous day with the result that at the last moment the route originally planned had been drastically shortened. The only drawback to the shortened route was that it took the procession past the School of Law, a hotbed of nationalism, where the students would certainly have demonstrated had they not been sent home for the day and the buildings locked. Even so, Owen had been a little apprehensive. The hazard had been safely negotiated, however, and now, with the Bab-el-Louk turned, the end was in sight.

There was the Royal Carriage, with the plumes and tufted lances of the Royal Guard riding alongside. Owen had strongly advocated this arrangement, not on the grounds of their fighting qualities but because there was a better chance of them intercepting a bullet meant for the royal pair. So far as military action went, he had a great deal more faith in the Duke of Cornwall's Light Infantry, a point which had not escaped the Welsh Fusiliers when they had suggested them for the Guard of Honour.

The Fusiliers were standing a little to the right of Owen, lining both sides of the street at the entrance to Abdin Square. They were placing bets on how many of the Light Infantry would collapse before the procession reached the cool harbour of the Palace grounds.

'Two gaps second rank from the rear—there must be more than that!'

'They've closed ranks. At least four!'

'No, no, I make it six!'

'There's another going to go at any moment—there he goes!'

One of the Fusiliers stepped out and dragged him into the side out of the way of the horses.

'You're all right now, mate. Just lie there. You're well out of it. They'll be marking time in the square for the next half hour.'

The rest of the escort went past. With the exception of the Light Infantry, they were all from the Egyptian Army, and very picturesque they looked: the Mounted Camel Brigade, the Mounted Horse, the Sudanese infantry with their tall red fezzes and their long bayonets, sundry Egyptian regiments under the Khedive's banner.

Meanwhile, the British soldiers lined the streets, their sun helmets blocking the view for the crowd massed behind them.

The Royal Carriage swept at last into the Square, the Khedive waving a royal hand, the Grand Duke inclining a ducal back. The Guard closed in around it. As the other detachments came into the Square they took up positions to the left and right until eventually the royal carriage was barely visible.

The Fusiliers had been right. The Guard had to mark time while the rest of the escort was deploying into the Square. Two more Light Infantry fell over.

At last the Royal Carriage rumbled forward and entered the Palace gates, the Light Infantry now running behind, with the Royal Guard still strung alongside. The detachments in the Square came to a halt.

ᘒ

'Very satisfactory,' said Shearer at the debriefing next day.

'Casualties?'

'About fifty down with sunstroke, sir.'

'Oh, not bad!' said the major.

'All British?' asked Paul.

'If we exclude what went on in the cafés and bars last night,' said Owen.

'Understandable reaction,' said the major hastily. 'Men been on parade since dawn.'

'But I thought Captain Shearer still held responsibility? Until midnight?'

'I don't feel, sir,' said Shearer unhappily, 'that we should abandon the concept of unified policing just because of this one instance—'

'Unified policing?' said Paul. 'Ah, yes, but under whom?'

'I think the Army has shown what it can do, sir.'

'But the crucial arrest, I understood, took place on water. Now, I believe the views of the Navy are—'

ᘓᙏᓼᓚ

'Again, perhaps?' murmured Zeinab.

'Certainly,' said Owen.

ᘓᙏᓼᓚ

Afterwards, Zeinab was disposed to chat.

'I could, I suppose, become an opera singer,' she said.

'You've got everything it takes,' said Owen encouragingly. 'Bar the voice, of course.'

'Does that really matter?' asked Zeinab. 'Couldn't I hire a claque? Oh, of course, I was forgetting! That would cost money and rather destroy the point.'

'What point?' asked Owen drowsily. 'Why do you want to become an opera singer, anyway?'

'To make money.'

'What's happened to the allowance from your father?'

'Nothing's happened to it. I just need more, that's all.'

'What for?'

'To support you.'

'Support *me*?' said Owen, waking up. 'Why are you going to have to do that?'

'Well, you're certainly not going to support me, are you? Not on the pitiful pay you get.'

Owen knew where he was now. Zeinab was talking about marriage. Or was she? Seriously? As opposed to merely entertaining the idea? Zeinab liked, he knew, to entertain the idea of marriage, especially in moments of tenderness; but that was not quite the same as really thinking about it. When they really thought about it, they tended to shy away from the sheer difficulty of the whole business. Zeinab at these moments took refuge behind such apparently practical problems as where would they find enough money to live on. For Owen, who never thought about money anyway, that wasn't the problem at all. What was the problem was how a British official could marry an Egyptian and stay in his job, particularly a job as sensitive as that of the Mamur Zapt. What effect would it have on his career? And what, come to think of it, was happening to his career anyway? In British service overseas you retired early. You'd hardly got there before they were heaving you out. Wherever you were going to get to, you had to get there quick. Had he already got there? If so, what had happened to that period of affluence which he had always supposed would intervene between impecunious apprenticeship and equally impecunious superannuation? With these and similar considerations it was easy to deflect the more serious issues which clustered around their relationship.

Entertaining the idea of marriage, as opposed to seriously facing it, was, perhaps, what they both did. It occurred to him that Zeinab had been entertaining the idea rather more often lately. God, what did that mean—?

He stole a glance at her as she lay beside him. Relaxed, now, she lay back comfortably with a half smile on her lips.

He was thoroughly awake now. God, this was serious. He had some real thinking to do. What would the Consul-

General say? What the Khedive? Would it have to go to the Secretary of State? How would they manage? If he had to get another job? What job? But he would do it if she asked him. Wait a minute: wasn't that the wrong way round? Oughtn't he to be asking her? God, this was serious, much more serious than Grand Dukes or any of that stuff, you could massacre the whole damned lot for all he cared. This was serious!

Or was it? Highly satisfied, Zeinab lay back and enjoyed the game.

⚬⟋⟋⟍⟍⚬

It was the very last engagement of the Grand Duke's visit.

The Fusiliers stood stiff and straight in the Grand Hall of the Palace.

'Services to the Tsar!' intoned the Russian Chargé.

The Grand Duke pinned on another medal. He came to the end of the line.

'Captain Owen, sir,' whispered the Chargé.

'Order of Saint Vasili and Saint Vladimir!'

'Well deserved!' said the Grand Duke. 'Well deserved! What was it for?' he whispered to the Chargé.

'Suppressing the Mingrelian Conspiracy,' said the Chargé.

To receive a free catalog of other Poisoned Pen Press titles,
please contact us in one of the following ways:

Phone: 1-800-421-3976
Facsimile: 1-480-949-1707
Email: info@poisonedpenpress.com
Website: www.poisonedpenpress.com

Poisoned Pen Press
6962 E. First Ave. Ste 103
Scottsdale, AZ 85251